RIFLED GOLD

Center Point
Large Print

Also by W. C. Tuttle and available from Center Point Large Print:

The Mystery of the Red Triangle
The Valley of Vanishing Herds

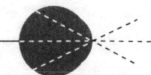

**This Large Print Book carries the
Seal of Approval of N.A.V.H.**

RIFLED GOLD

W. C. Tuttle

CENTER POINT LARGE PRINT
THORNDIKE, MAINE

CHAPTER I

THE COWPUNCHERS OF DISASTER

The first telegram was sent to Elene Corey, Chicago, Illinois. It had been dispatched by her mother, from Painted Wells, Arizona, and, with the brevity common to tragedy, it read:

> YOUR FATHER KILLED TODAY
> ADVISE YOU COME AT ONCE

A second was to Cornelius Van Avery, Phoenix, Arizona:

> ABSOLUTELY OPPOSED TO ANY
> SUCH AN IDEA STOP
> QUIT PLAYING THE FOOL AND
> COME HOME

This message came from Pittsburgh, and was signed: 'Father.'

Also a telegram was sent by the secretary of the Cattlemen's Association of Arizona, addressed to Hashknife Hartley . . .

Elene Corey wired one word: 'Coming.'

Cornelius Van Avery's answer to his father was:

5

Hashknife Hartley did not answer his wire.

Sleepy Stevens, Hashknife's partner, was susceptible to beauty. Just now he was aware that the prettiest girl he had ever seen was sitting across the aisle from him. She was wearing a dark dress unrelieved by any other color. Her hair had a coppery sheen in the train lights, and there was a sober sadness in her big eyes. Sleepy wondered how she would look if she smiled.

Sleepy was undeniably a cowboy. A battered Stetson lay on his lap; his gray trousers were tucked into the tops of well-worn, high-heeled boots. He was of average height, wide of shoulder, and slightly bow-legged. His face was blocky and deeply graved, his mouth wide above a firm chin. His eyes were of a peculiar blue—innocent-looking eyes which seemed to regard the world with surprise.

Seated beside Sleepy was Hashknife Hartley, half asleep. At least he appeared half asleep. Hashknife was several inches over six feet in height, lean and lank as a greyhound. His face was thin with prominent cheekbones, a generous nose, and a wide, thin-lipped mouth. His hair was a sandy roan color and badly in need of trimming. One damp lock habitually dropped down to intersect his right eyebrow. His garb was much the same as that of Sleepy.

On the opposite seat were their warbags—the valises of cowboys—in which they carried their worldly goods.

Outside was the moonlit panorama of the passing Arizona scenery.

Sleepy nudged Hashknife, who opened his eyes quickly and glanced sidewise at him.

'Huh?' he grunted vacantly.

'She almost smiled,' whispered Sleepy.

'Who?'

'Across the aisle,' replied Sleepy. 'Gosh, didja ever see one that was prettier?'

Hashknife sighed and shifted his position.

'I hope you fall in love someday,' said Sleepy.

'No, you don't.' Hashknife yawned and looked at his watch.

'I wish somethin' would happen to give me a chance to speak to her.' Sleepy spoke his thought aloud.

The station whistle of the engine came drifting back to them, and in a few moments the train began to slacken speed. A brakeman, carrying a lantern, came through the car, going toward the front.

'What station is this?' asked Sleepy.

'Porcupine—a flag station. Don't stop here once a month,' mumbled the brakeman as he hurried on.

Hashknife glanced at a folder which had been well-thumbed.

'We've got ten miles more, Sleepy.'

'Is that all?' Sleepy sighed, looking at the girl across the aisle.

Only ten miles more, and another pretty girl would pass out of his life. Sleepy's love-affairs usually lasted just about that long.

The train drew to a clanking stop. Into the car stumbled a man carrying two heavy pieces of baggage. He wore his big five-gallon Stetson jerked down over one eye, and he was panting from exertion as he staggered aboard.

Crash! The lower half of a window splintered, and from the depot platform came the crack of a revolver.

The passenger from Porcupine sat down heavily in the aisle, with both valises on his lap, as the train pulled out. He cocked his head to one side and looked with fear at the broken window. The lights of the station faded out before he got to his feet.

He was a young man, not much past his majority, and too fair of skin to belong in this country. His well-shaped head was covered with damp blond curls. His clothes were an expensive mixture; well-tailored, but the trousers were tucked into a pair of the gaudiest cowboy boots the two cowboys had ever seen. He stood up in them awkwardly and looked at the three people in the car.

'That shot didn't hit you, did it?' asked Hashknife.

'No, sir,' said the young man seriously. 'I think it hit my baggage. May I sit down?'

'You've got a ticket, haven't you?' Sleepy grinned.

'No, sir, I haven't. You see, I—I did not have time to purchase one.'

'Jist flew and 'lighted, eh?' Sleepy was still grinning as the young man took the seat behind the lady.

'Yes, I imagine that was it. Sorry to arrive that way, but I—you see, I had no choice.'

The brakeman came through, crunched some of the glass with his heel as he went down the aisle, and stopped short to glance at the broken window.

'What busted the window?' he asked; then he added, before anyone might answer, 'Wasn't that a shot fired in Porcupine?'

'Mebbe it was a drunken cowboy,' suggested Hashknife.

'Yeah, I suppose it was. Darn fool might have hurt somebody.'

The brakeman kicked the glass out of the aisle and went on. The young man leaned over the back of the seat, and the girl turned to look at him.

'I'm sorry if it frightened you,' he said. 'I really wasn't to blame.'

'It was perfectly all right,' replied the girl calmly, and Sleepy wanted to applaud her.

'You see, there was a poker game,' explained the young man. 'I was looking at some ranch property which did not suit me.'

He took a deep breath and laughed softly.

'I really do not know one cow from another, and all land looks like just dirt to me. But the poker game—I really believe it was started to cheat me out of some money. You see, we each bought a thousand dollars' worth of chips. There were two cowboys and a saloon-keeper. He—the saloon-keeper—staked the two cowboys. I had two aces, clubs and spades, and I also had the king of clubs and two little clubs. Well, I was inclined to draw one card to the flush, but decided to draw to my two aces.

'I drew a pair of sevens, which made me two pair, and I bet all the chips I had. Well, one of the cowboys had three kings, and one of the kings was clubs. I searched the deck, but was unable to find more than one king of clubs.'

He drew another deep breath and continued:

'I had heard that it is dangerous to accuse a cowboy of cheating; so I—I drew my gun and made them give me back my thousand dollars. Then I backed out, secured my baggage at the hotel, and I just did catch this train.'

The girl looked across at Hashknife and Sleepy, who were gazing upon the young man with undisguised amazement.

'I think you did very well,' she said dryly.

'Do you?' he asked eagerly. 'That is certainly fine of you.'

The conductor did not notice the broken window, but came straight to the young man.

'Ticket, please,' he said gruffly.

'Ticket? Oh, yes. No, I haven't any ticket, but I have money,' he said, drawing out a roll of bills.

'Red Hill is the next station,' said the conductor. 'Be there in five minutes now.'

The girl stood up and began closing a valise.

'How far are you going?' asked the conductor of the young man.

'Oh, yes.' The young man scratched his cheek thoughtfully. 'Take out the fare from Porcupine to Red Hill, Conductor.'

'All right. That will exactly empty this car.'

The young man leaned over and spoke to Hashknife—

'Is that your destination too?'

'Seems to be.' The tall cowboy smiled.

'Isn't that fine! Why, this is a regular party. I'm glad I came.'

The girl stood up and reached for a suitcase on the rack above the window, but the young man sprang on his seat and lifted it down.

'May I assist you with this?' he asked seriously.

Hashknife reached across and took it from him. Before the young man could voice a protest, Hashknife said:

'You get off the rear of this train, young man; we'll handle all the baggage.'

'But I don't see—'

'Mebbe you forget there's telegraph wires in this country. Drop off and keep out of sight for a few minutes.'

The young man was not exactly a fool, and he grasped Hashknife's meaning. They were nearing Red Hill. Hashknife picked up the girl's valise and one belonging to the young man, who walked swiftly back through the coaches as the train slowed.

As they came to the doorway, they saw a man running beside the train. He was there as they came down to the platform—a big, squareheaded man, with the lights from the train flashing on the sheriff's emblem on his vest. He glanced sharply at the girl and the two cowboys, decided that none of them answered the description, then sprang into the coach.

He was running through the train as it started, and they saw him make a quick leap from the rear coach. His intentions were to land on the end of the high depot platform, but he miscalculated about six feet, and they saw him go end over end down an embankment and disappear in the darkness.

Hashknife chuckled and turned to the girl.

'Where are you goin'?' he asked.

'There is only one hotel here,' she said.

'You've been here before?'

'My home is at Painted Wells.'

'Yeah? Well, I reckon we might as well go to that hotel.'

There was little illumination on the main street of Red Hill, but they had no trouble in finding the New York Hotel. And in the diminutive lobby they found the young man again, arguing with the whiskered proprietor about a room with bath.

'Well, howdy, Miss Corey!' exclaimed the old man, holding out his hand. 'By Golly, it's shore good to see you. Thought you was in—oh, yeah, I done forgot about your pa.'

The girl's eyes filled with tears, but she smiled gamely. The young man looked inquiringly at her.

'Well, now, I'll give you a front room, Miss Corey,' said the proprietor nervously. 'Reckon you're tired plumb out. You come with me, and the rest of you fellers'll have to wait.'

He took the girl's baggage and went up the rickety stairs ahead of her.

At the landing the girl turned.

'Thank you for carrying my bags,' she said to Hashknife.

'You're shore welcome, Miss Corey.'

'What a girl!' said the young man softly. He turned to Hashknife. 'My name is Cornelius Van Avery,' he said.

'Mine's Hartley.' Hashknife smiled, and introduced Sleepy.

'You better git into a room pretty quick,' advised Sleepy. 'That sheriff done a high dive off that train, and I'm bettin' he ain't in no condition to see anythin' funny in the world.'

'Thank you very much for helping me. I never thought they would telegraph. What do you suppose they told the sheriff?'

'That you held 'em up,' replied Hashknife dryly. 'You did, didn't you?'

'Well, I suppose I did—yes,' he said, laughing. 'And I lost my gun when I climbed into the train. I suppose I can buy another here.'

'Why do you need a gun?'

'Well, it came in handy once.'

'Shore. Next time your luck might change. I'd advise you to grow up to fit the country before you start packin' hardware.'

'Thanks,' dryly. 'But you forget that the sheriff is after me.'

Hashknife laughed and shook his head.

'Van Avery, if that sheriff ever recognizes you, hold up your hands. The law will give you an even break, but an Arizona sheriff don't take chances.'

The old man came back and assigned their rooms.

'No bath?' queried Van Avery.

'Not unless you git in a waterin'-trough,

14

young feller. Hell, you don't look so awful dirty!'

'Don't folks around here take baths?'

'Well, I ain't never seen none of 'em in the act.'

'I suppose I can stand it.'

'What time does the stage leave for Painted Wells?' asked Hashknife.

'Nine o'clock sharp, if the driver's sober.'

'Thanks.'

'Are you going to Painted Wells?' asked Van Avery.

'Shore,' drawled Sleepy.

'Miss Corey is goin' too,' offered the old man. 'Her pa was killed sev'ral days ago up there. She's been to Chicago, studyin' for to be somethin'—I dunno what.'

'Call me at eight in the morning,' said Van Avery, and they went clattering up the stairs to their rooms.

'What do you make of Cornelius?' Sleepy asked as the two cowboys undressed.

'He's good for a laugh,' replied Hashknife, his eyes twinkling. 'Can you imagine him pullin' a gun and takin' his money back? Stickin' up two punchers and a gambler! Sleepy, there must be somethin' that looks out for babies and fools. And the fact that the sheriff is lookin' for him don't faze him a bit, 'cause he don't realize that they'd send him over the road for what he done tonight.'

'Oh, shore.' Sleepy laughed. 'Fools draw guns, where gunmen set on their hands and keep still.

That Miss Corey is shore pretty, and she belongs in Painted Wells. Now jist what in hell do you suppose they wanted us to go to Painted Wells for? No information—jist go there.'

'Probably don't amount to much,' replied Hashknife, yanking at a recalcitrant boot.

'Mysterious stuff!' snorted Sleepy. 'They knowed you'd go. If they come right out and told you what it was all about, you'd prob'ly turn down the job. Anyway, I don't hanker for no Cattle Association work—not openly. Ain't worth the risk. Someday they'll be sayin':

' "Oh, yeah, I remember them two fellers. They got snagged on a couple hot bullets. Too bad."

'That's what they'll be sayin', and we'll be, as Adobe Ed calls 'em, a couple skillingtons. I asked Ed what a skillington was, and he said it was a man with his insides out and his outsides off.'

Hashknife laughed as he took his belt and holstered gun from his warbag and hung them on the bedpost.

'We'll see about pickin' up a couple broncs in the mornin',' he said.

'And not go on the stage?'

'Not if we can get broncs.'

'Pshaw!'

'Thinkin' about ridin' with Miss Corey?'

'Allus somebody takin' the joy out of my life,'

16

complained Sleepy, as he crawled between the blankets. 'I wonder if the sheriff will be watchin' for Cornelius?'

'No,' replied Hashknife, 'he thinks Cornelius is still on that train, unless he wired to the next town to pick him up, and I don't believe he'd do that. Probably wire back to Porcupine and tell 'em there wasn't no such a person on that train. From the position he was in the last we saw, he likely rubbed his nose off on the cinders.'

'How far is it to Painted Wells?' asked Sleepy.

'Hadn't ought to be more than fifteen, twenty miles.'

'Hope it's a hundred and fifty.'

'Why?'

'Be easier to take the stage than to ride a strange horse.'

Hashknife blew out the light.

In the cold light of day, Red Hill was not a place of beauty. The main street was a sort of dog leg in shape; most of the false-fronted buildings were closed, the windows boarded. The drop in the market price of copper had made Red Hill what it was this day—a semi-ghost town, just struggling along without any visible means of support.

Red Hill had once been a copper producer, while Painted Wells, fifteen miles to the north, had been only a cow-town—until a big gold strike had been made. There were still plenty of cattle on the Painted Wells Range, but gold was the big thing.

Across the street from the New York Hotel was the Elite Saloon, a big place which had flourished in the palmy days of Red Hill. At the bar stood Banty Brayton, the sheriff, and Handsome Hartwig, his deputy. The sheriff was a big man, grizzled, with a scraggly mustache adorning his serious face.

Handsome Hartwig was five feet six in height, broad of beam, with the champion bowlegs of the county. Handsome had a bullet-shaped head, weary blue eyes, scarcely any eyebrows, a long, rubicund nose, and a mouth which seemed to extend almost from ear to ear.

'No, I'll tell you what happened to him, Ez'ry,' Handsome said to the bartender. 'One of them squawk-mouthed waddies down in Porcupine sent Banty a telegram las' night, sayin' that a feller had stuck up their poker game, took away plenty *dinero*, and made a getaway on the train. Banty, bein' one of them there Arizony sheriffs what allus gits his man, hopped the train when it pulls in and gallops the whole len'th of the train, askin' everybody if they was from Porcupine. They wasn't, and then—'

'Never no such a damn thing!' growled Banty. 'What I done—'

'The train was pullin' out,' continued Handsome, 'and Banty runs to the rear end, where

18

he thinks he sees this here bandit goin' down a gopher hole at the end of the platform; so Banty ups and does himself a dive after this here hole-huntin' jigger.'

'No such a damn thing,' corrected the sheriff wearily.

'Well, look at his face, if you don't believe me,' said Handsome. 'He ain't got no skin on his nose, one eyebrow's gone, and he'll shore have to use sheep dip on his chin if he ever raises any whiskers agin.'

'And you didn't git the holdup man, eh?' queried the bartender.

'Wasn't none,' said Handsome disgustedly. 'Can you imagine arrestin' a man for holdin' up a poker game in Porcupine? Mebbe he hijacked the gang, but that's all. Can you imagine that bunch gittin' up on a witness stand and swearin' that somebody robbed 'em?'

Banty gazed disconsolately at his glass.

'Bein' a sheriff ain't such a nice job,' offered the bartender.

'Nice!' Banty spat the word.

'I 'member how hard you worked to git elected,' said Handsome. 'You been sheriff less 'n a year, and you're sour on the job. I think she's a great job.'

'You be damned! What do you know about it? All you've done is to make fun of everythin'. You're a hell of a deputy!'

19

'I'm all right.'

'You ain't neither. Morally and physically you're a wreck. Financially, you ain't got nothin', and—'

'I'm all right physically.'

'With them bowlegs and that nose? You look like a cross between a anteater and a pair of ice-tongs.'

'Gee!' exclaimed Handsome softly. 'Well, I'm all right mentally, Banty.'

'You're crazy.'

'Well,'—Handsome sighed resignedly—'my heart is in the right place.'

'So's your gall.'

The sheriff sighed deeply and looked through the window. The Painted Wells stage was loading at the little stage office. Elene Corey and Cornelius Van Avery were on the sidewalk watching Mark Hawker, the driver, arranging his load. Van Avery was wearing his big hat and high-heeled boots. Handsome turned his head and looked.

'Ain't that Elene Corey?' he asked.

'I thought I seen her gittin' off the train last night,' grunted the sheriff. 'Go over and talk to her, Handsome.'

'Talk to her yourself,' retorted the deputy. 'Allus sluffin' the dirty work off on me.'

'Hawker's prob'ly told her,' said the bartender. 'Who's that fancy jigger with her?' wondered

Handsome. 'Do you reckon she brought that specimen from the East, Banty?'

'Looks like it.'

'That there Studson hat shore cost a hunk of *dinero*.'

'Dressed in black,' muttered the sheriff. 'Prob'ly heard a'ready.'

'Shore, she knows her pa is dead, 'cause her ma sent her a telegram.'

'Uh-huh. Betcher she don't know her brother-in-law is in jail for murder.'

'You ought to go over and tell her, Banty. You was the one what made the arrest.'

They moved over closer to the window and saw Elene and Van Avery climb up on the stage.

'Mebbe she got married,' said Handsome.

'Hope so,' said the sheriff. 'Prob'ly help you keep your mind on my business. You're bad enough normally, but if you ever fell in love I'd hate to see you—at your age.'

'I'm a young man yet.'

'Young! Why, you've got one foot in the grave and the other on a cake of soft soap. Let's have a drink.'

Cornelius Van Avery looked over Red Hill as they rode out of town.

'Quite a place,' he observed to Elene.

They were on the wide seat with Mark Hawker, who was viciously chewing tobacco and trying to keep his mind on the horses. He spat violently.

'Best danged town in Arizony!' he snorted.

'What is the population?' asked Van Avery.

'Thirty-five souls, six Chinamen, and about sixty Mexicans. Are you goin' to Painted Wells on business or pleasure?'

'Is it a good town?' asked Van Avery, ignoring the question.

'Best in Arizony. Ask Miss Corey; she was raised there. Her pa was killed there a few days ago. Pretty danged hot weather to keep a corpse, too.'

Van Avery shifted his eyes and looked at Elene. Her eyes were full of tears, but she shook her head at Van Avery, indicating that Hawker's remark was merely from ignorance and with no intent to hurt her feelings.

'Too bad about Ken Steele, wasn't it?' remarked Hawker.

'What about Ken?' asked Elene quickly.

'They've got him jailed for killin' your pa.'

'They've—you say Ken killed my father, Mark?'

'Yeah.'

'But—oh, that couldn't be! My God! Oh, poor Glad!'

Van Avery steadied her with a hand on her shoulder. He thought she was going to faint. They traveled along in silence for a long time. Elene was looking straight ahead with her hands clenched in her lap, trying to steady her nerves. Finally she turned to Van Avery.

'Ken Steele is my sister's husband,' she said. 'His father disowned him when he married my sister.'

'Was that so terrible?' asked Van Avery.

'His father is wealthy,' said Elene, 'and Ken owed lots of money. Glad wrote to me very often. Ken couldn't pay his debts on what he could make as a cowboy. He worked for my father. But he and Glad were very much in love.'

Hawker spat again.

'My the'ry is, too danged much Ed Ault,' he said.

Elene looked at the driver quickly.

'What do you mean?'

'What everybody knows, if they know anythin' a-tall. Ed Ault has been stuck on your sister for more 'n a year. He hated Ken Steele, 'cause Ken won her. Old Silver Steel refused to pay Ken's gamblin' debts, contendin' that Ken was of age, and Ault shore shut down on Ken real hard. Ken has that little home in town and he's got a few head of horses. Ault had the sheriff collect everythin' Ken owned.'

'But why blame Ed Ault? If Ken owed—'

'Well, he pushed Ken awful hard for money. He didn't collect everythin' Ken owned until after the murder. You see, your dad had a ten-thousand-dollar mortgage on his place with the bank. They refused to keep it a-runnin' any longer, and your dad was stuck for money. Him

23

and Ault has been friends a long time, and Ault loaned him the money to pay the bank, him a-takin' a note for a year.

'It happened about four o'clock in the afternoon, after the bank had done closed up, and your pa started home with the money. Ken was in the saloon and heard Ault and your pa talkin'; so he started out ahead of your pa. Now, I ain't a-sayin' who done it. Your pa had been hit over the head, prob'ly after he was shot; and the sheriff found Ken's gun in the brush near the spot. It had blood on it, and one shell had been spent.'

'And the money gone?' asked Elene huskily.

'Oh, shore. Ken shut his mouth tight, after he denied doin' the job; and they can't git nothin' out of him.'

The road was rather dangerous; so the driver ceased his discourse to handle the team. Finally he turned to Van Avery.

'Are you a drummer?' he asked.

'A drummer?' Van Avery laughed. 'No, I am no musician.'

'Hell!' snorted Hawker softly.

'Sorry,' said Van Avery. 'But I suppose I could beat a drum.'

'Are you jist smart or ignorant?' asked Hawker.

Van Avery flushed quickly.

'I don't believe my mental status is any of your business.'

'Your mental what?'

Van Avery shrugged his shoulders. Hawker glanced at Elene.

'This feller come from the East with you?' he asked.

'No one came from the East with me,' she replied evenly.

He turned to Van Avery.

'Kinda new in this country, ain'tcha?'

'You are considered a good driver, are you not?' countered Van Avery.

'I shore am.'

'Well, stop your cross-examination and confine yourself to driving.'

Hawker scratched the back of his neck, spat copiously and studied the road ahead, where it led through the sandy bed of a dry wash. The heavy stage lurched along through the ruts and up the bank, where it ran through a grove of giant saguaro cactus and a heavy growth of ocotillo. As they swung around a curve, the lead horses swerved wildly from the road, yanking the heavy wheels out of the ruts and causing the driver to jerk frantically on the lines.

All was confusion for a moment. Van Avery was nearly thrown from the seat. They recovered only to see two masked men, guns in hand, one at the head of a lead horse, the other near the right front wheel of the stage. Hawker's hands were high above his head, and the other two lost no time in emulating his example.

'You can take down your hands,' said the man near the wheel, 'and throw down the money-box.' His gun shifted quickly to Van Avery. 'Keep your hands up, *hombre*! I'm speakin' to the driver.'

'She's empty today,' replied Hawker dryly.

'Throw it down.'

Hawker tossed down the money-box.

'Get down—all of you.'

They lost no time in obeying orders. The other bandit came toward them.

'Search 'em,' said the spokesman huskily. 'Never mind the lady.'

Van Avery shifted his feet, with no intention of interfering with the robbery, but as quick as a flash the spokesman fired. Van Avery cried out sharply as he jerked back, seemed to catch his heel, and fell backward, striking his head on the hub of the wheel.

Van Avery was down, his body motionless.

'Damn fool to reach for a gun,' growled the killer.

'He hasn't any gun,' said Elene. 'You never gave him a chance, you murdering brute.'

The killer laughed harshly.

'You talk like a native, ma'am.'

'Want me to go through him?' asked the other bandit. 'Better make it fast.'

'Let him go. You two pile on to that stage and head out of here.'

'Won't you put him on the stage?' asked Elene.

'To hell with him. Git up there and git out. Driver, you hit the grit and don't look back.'

'How about that money-box—it's empty.'

'Leave it here. We'll judge that end of it. Now, travel!'

Hawker was no fool. He lashed the team, and the stage went rocking on toward Painted Wells. Elene glanced back as they struck the next curve in the road; but the two bandits had gone and Van Avery was still there.

'Stop the team, will you?' she asked Hawker.

'What for?' he asked, making no effort to comply with her wishes.

'Let me off and give me your gun.'

Hawker looked narrowly at her.

'Don't be a fool. The sheriff and deputy was in Red Hill when we left, and they'll find him.'

'It may be hours before they come along.'

'It'll be all the same to that tenderfoot. He never knew what hit him. Who was he, anyway?'

'What difference does that make? At least, he is a gentleman.'

'Mebbe he *was*. Don't be so danged upset. He wasn't anythin' to you.'

'They shot him down for no reason at all.'

'Thought he was tryin' to draw a gun.'

'I tell you he had no gun.'

'Well, it's none of my business. I'm paid to drive a stage, not to swap lead with holdup men. There wasn't no money in that box.'

• • •

The dust of the disappearing stage had hardly settled when Van Avery opened his eyes and blinked up at the top of a saguaro. He was conscious of a dull ache in his head and a great thirst. The bright sun, slanting down past the saguaro top, hurt his eyes. He started to turn over, but became conscious of another pain which seemed to be connected in some way with his ribs on the left side.

With no clear understanding of anything, he sat up, winked rapidly, swallowed thickly, and wondered what sort of dream this might be. He was sitting in the middle of a dusty road; that much was certain. There seemed to be a number of those queer-looking, tall cacti surrounding him. He rubbed his head and began collecting his thoughts. His left side interested him, and, after feeling around, he discovered that his fingers were sticky with blood.

And then his memory came back like a shot. He remembered everything now. There had been two masked men. Now they were gone, and the stage was gone.

There was a stinging sensation in his side, but his head hurt even worse. It was bleeding a little, and there was a lump the size of an egg just above his right ear.

His big Stetson hat was still on the ground where it had fallen. He finally got to his feet, fought back the dizziness, put on his hat and tilted it down over his left ear. His sense of direction was faulty, but he reasoned that either direction would take him to a town; so he started bravely toward Painted Wells. He was weakly staggering when Banty Brayton and Handsome Hartwig overtook him.

They recognized him as the young man who had climbed aboard the stage at Red Hill, but they asked no questions. Handsome always carried a small canteen of water on his saddle, and he also had a bottle of something stronger in his chaps pocket. He gave Van Avery a generous drink of both and set him down in the shade.

'This jigger has shore been bumped,' declared Handsome.

'Blood there on his shirt,' said Banty. 'Mebbe been shot.'

'Been shot?' queried Handsome.

'I—I think so,' whispered Van Avery. 'More water, please.'

'Shore; wet the old neck and then lemme see that side.'

Examination proved that Van Avery had been shot. The bullet had furrowed the flesh and skidded off a rib, but had done little real damage. The shock had knocked him down, and his head hitting the hub of the wheel had caused the shooter to consider the shot a bull's-eye.

'How do you feel?' asked the sheriff.

'Fine,' lied Van Avery. 'Where's the stage?'

'What happened to you, anyway?'

'Two masked men held us up.'

'Lovely dove!' exclaimed Handsome. 'One of 'em shoot you?'

'I suppose that is what occurred.'

'Why did he shoot you?'

'I haven't the slightest idea.'

The sheriff snorted disgustedly and turned to the horses.

'Double up with him on your horse, Handsome.' And to Van Avery, 'You ride a horse, don'tcha?'

'If they are gentle.'

'Oh, yeah. Well, git into that saddle of mine, and I'll ride behind you. My bronc won't buck much—not with my weight on his rump.'

Van Avery tried to mount on the right side of the horse; but Handsome led him around and helped him into the saddle. The horse made a strenuous objection to the sheriff; but the big man, handling the reins from the rear, spurred the animal into the road and let it run a few hundred yards with the double burden, after which it was willing to adopt a slower gait.

'Feelin' all right, kid?' asked the sheriff.

'My name is Cornelius Van Avery.'

'I reckon that'll hold you for a while.' Handsome laughed.

The sheriff squinted thoughtfully as he considered the back of Van Avery's head.

'Did you come from Porcupine last night?' he asked.

'Yes, sir,' replied Van Avery.

'You did, eh? I hear you stuck up a poker game down there.'

'Did you hear about that, too? I discarded a king of clubs, and one of them stole it. I—I made them give me back my money, and then I—I—'

'Oh, oh!' yelled Handsome. 'Grab him, Banty! Why, the son of a gun fainted. That's it, hold him up straight. Let him lean agin you. He's lost quite a lot of blood, I'll betcha. Can you handle him all right?'

'Shore, he can't fall.'

'Well, I'll be a horned toad! So that's the jigger that held up them thieves in Porcupine! Stole his discards, eh? Yeah, that sounds like gospel truth to me. And you ain't goin' to arrest him for it either, Banty.'

'Who said I was? Keep still about him bein' the feller. He ain't got no more business bein' in Arizona than I have bein' President.'

'You ought to adopt him, Banty. Give you somethin' to do. Take him at that tender age, and you might even train him to catch rustlers, holdup men, and higraders. I'd take a chance, if I was you. But git him a name. Don't let him grow up answerin' to the name of Cornelius. Imagine a couple parents hamstringin' a kid thataway.

'Cor-neil-yus! Sounds like a bullet glancin' off

a rock, if you say it real quick. Might call him Corny. But him bein' sort of a sorrel, we might call him Blondy. Yeah, I'd vote for Blondy. You better hold him up straighter. You wouldn't want the poor critter to git a perm'nent kink in his neck and have to spend the rest of his life lookin' at them boots of his'n, would you?'

'Them are purty boots,' said Banty.

'Yeah, they are. Betcha they cost fifty dollars. Him a-wearin' fifty-dollar boots and a million-dollar hat, tryin' to mount a bronc from the wrong side! I hope he don't die on your hands, Banty. Looks to me as though he was leakin' a lot of blood.'

'Aw, he's all right. Old Doc Smedley will fix him up fine.'

'Yeah, I betcha he will. Prob'ly probe him len'thwise for that bullet, which ain't in him. That's how Old Smed learned anatomy. If you go to him with a cut finger, the first thing he does is examine you for stringhalt and ringbone. Yeah, he may fix Blondy up all right, but by the time he's through with the treatment, poor Blondy will nicker instead of laugh. I 'member the time Old Smed treated me for indigestion. Three days later a paper blowed across the room, and I kicked the door off the hinges. Don't tell me he wasn't a horse doctor before he came to Painted Wells.'

'May I have a drink of water?' asked Van Avery hoarsely.

'Whiskey or water?' asked Handsome.

'Water, please.'

'Doc's got a job on his hands,' said Handsome seriously.

Hashknife and Sleepy had shipped their saddles, bridles, and chaps to Red Hill, and they had little difficulty in securing a pair of horses from a trader. Hashknife spent an hour with the proprietor of the hotel, trying to get some information about Painted Wells; something which would account for the Cattle Association's sending him and Sleepy there on a blind trail.

'Feller named Steele—Old Silver, they calls him—owns most of the biggest mine up there,' offered the hotel man. 'Calls it Comanche Chief. Free millin' gold mine, and a good producer. Steele also owns the JS cow outfit. That there girl who went out on the stage was born up there at Painted Wells. Daddy's name was Milt Corey, and a nicer feller you never did see. But a few days ago his son-in-law gunned him to death, they say. They got Ken Steele in jail, and they say it looks bad agin him.'

'Is this Ken Steele a son of Silver Steele?' asked Hashknife.

'Shore is. Ain't never been no friendship between Milt Corey and Silver Steele. But Corey's daughter runs away and marries Steele's son, and it made Steele so damn mad that he throwed the kid out. Then the kid went to work for Corey, punchin' cows; and I thought everythin' was all right. They tell me that Old Milt had ten thousand dollars on him when he was killed, and the money was gone when they found him.'

All of which was not enlightening to Hashknife, because, checking up on dates, Corey had been killed late in the afternoon of the same day in which Hashknife had received the telegram in the morning. There was no hint of any cattle-rustling or horse-stealing. The old hotel man would have known if there had been, because he seemed to know everything else.

'I reckon we'll jist have to go to Painted Wells and stay there long enough to find out what is wrong,' said Hashknife. 'It's a cinch we're not there to investigate this Corey murder; and that's about all the old man knows anythin' about.'

'Anyway'—Sleepy smiled—'the road runs north, and there's hills to cross.'

'And a pretty girl in Painted Wells,' added Hashknife.

'And then some more hills,' said Sleepy seriously. 'Me and you always a-driftin', and more hills ahead.'

Hashknife looked wistfully at his partner.

'We're a queer pair, Sleepy. We're like the bear in that old song, who went over the mountain to see what he could see. And we've seen a lot of things, us two.'

'And nothin' to show for it,' said Sleepy.

'I dunno,' remarked Hashknife thoughtfully. 'Who has more? What would we do with money? Suppose you had a million, Sleepy.'

'Oh, I could git along on half that much. Have a couple of new heels put on my boots, a new cinch on my saddle, and I'd shore buy you a new vest, Hashknife.'

'Make damn dudes out of both of us, eh? That's what money does to you. No, we're better off thisaway.'

Perhaps the pretty girl was some inducement to Sleepy, but it was the lure of a strange place—the other side of the hill—that beckoned these two cowboys on. Always the hills called to them; and always there were more hills beyond these hills, and the call was ever the same.

Henry—Hashknife—Hartley, son of an itinerant minister of the Gospel, began life in the Milk River country of Montana. He was a cowpoke at ten and a top hand at sixteen. The wage of a range sky pilot is small; and the long, gangling, gray-eyed kid was obliged to make his own way.

Even at that age the hills called, and he drifted across Montana, Idaho, Washington, and the cattle ranges of Oregon. There were hills to the south, and he wandered to the land of manzanita, down through the painted country. Ten years of wandering brought him to the old Hashknife outfit, where he met Dave—Sleepy—Stevens, another cowboy with an itching foot, who had wandered from the south of Idaho.

And here was formed the partnership which Sleepy designated as the 'Cowpunchers of Disaster.' Together they rode away to see what might be on the other side of the hill. No place claimed them for long. Winter or summer, they kept heading for the hills, wondering what Fate had in store for them on the other side.

Back of Hashknife's level gray eyes was the brain of a detective—the ability to piece out a dim trail where others had failed. As Sleepy had said, 'Give him a dog track and he'll find a elephant.'

Working for the law had no appeal for them. They were not man-hunters. At rare times they would do a bit of detective work for a cattle association; but it irked them to accept such an assignment. They wanted to be free. And the secretary of this particular association knew this. That was why he merely asked them to go to Painted Wells. It left an element of mystery which he knew would interest Hashknife.

Sleepy never stopped to analyze anything. He had a blind faith in Hashknife's ability, a ready gun and the nerve of a fatalist. Many a time Fate had choked them with powder fumes and hot bullets had sung a death song past their ears; but the same Fate had left them unscathed. Death had struck at them from beside trails, lashed out at them in the dark; but they kept riding on, like the cowboy of that old range song:

Oh, I'll eat when I'm hungry,
I'll drink when I'm dry;
If a horse don't fall on me,
I'll live till I die.

CHAPTER II
THE TENDERFOOT

Handsome Hartwig, tilted back at the sheriff's desk, his feet on its top, gazed complacently at Silver Steele.

The big rancher and mine-owner sat slumped in an armchair, his sombrero on the floor beside him. Steele was square-jawed, with a face like hewn granite and a huge mane of silver-white hair. He wore tailored suits, which were never pressed after they left the tailor. His trousers were tucked into the tops of his boots. He invariably held the stump of a half-smoked cigar in one corner of his mouth.

'No, I didn't want to see Ken,' he said gruffly.

'All right.' Handsome nodded.

Steele scowled at the floor for several moments. Then, looking quizzically at Handsome, he said:

'Just how much evidence have they got against him?'

'Two times two makes four,' replied Handsome.

Steele grunted audibly and shifted his feet.

'Ken won't talk, eh?'

Handsome yawned.

'I reckon he ain't got nothin' to say.'

Ensued a period of silence, broken by Steele.

'What do you make of that holdup and the shootin' of the tenderfoot?'

'That was kinda funny, Steele. Doc Smedley's still patchin' up that feller. Another queer thing—that feller swears somebody stole two thousand dollars off him while he was knocked out.'

'Two thousand? That's a lot of money, Handsome.'

'I'd think so if it was mine. He says his name's Cornelius Van Avery. Can you imagine a man makin' a confession like that? I can't.'

The sheriff came in, nodded shortly to Steele, and sat down.

'We were discussin' Van Avery,' said Handsome.

The sheriff snorted and reached for his pipe.

'Ain't you goin' to try and catch the men who held up the stage and shot him?' asked Steele.

'Catch 'em!' grunted the sheriff. 'How'd you catch 'em? They've got the whole State of Arizona to git away in, ain't they? And if that ain't big enough, they can find another State, or head south to Mexico. You ain't been readin' detective stories, have you, Silver?'

'I'd like to see some action,' said Steele impatiently. He moved his chair over close to the desk and lowered his voice.

'I'm puttin' my cards on the table,' he said evenly. 'Do you remember Jack Cherry?'

'You mean the drunken prospector who fell

39

into a prospect hole and broke his neck?' asked the sheriff.

'He wasn't a prospector and he wasn't drunk, Banty. His name was Jack Payzant, and he was a detective. He never drank.'

The two officers looked queerly at each other. They remembered the incident very well. In fact, they had taken the dead man out of the prospect hole a week after he had died; so there was no reason for either of them to forget him.

'There was a bottle half full of whiskey,' said Handsome.

Steele nodded grimly.

'They made it look good. I hired Payzant to find out who was higradin' my ore, and I think he found out. But he never had a chance to tell me.'

'Your own miners must be stealin' the stuff,' said the sheriff.

'How do they get rid of it? How does it get out of the country? Who extracts the gold? Payzant probably worked on that angle. I tell you, I'm losing a lot of money every month. Who the devil can I trust? I've got men on every shift, watchin' everybody. How do I know my spies are honest? I don't; I'm takin' a chance.'

'If it was horse-stealin' or cattle-rustlin'—' began the sheriff.

'Hell!' raged Steele. 'One man can carry the price of several cows in his overall pocket and not show much of a bulge. Right now I'm workin' jewelry ore; but if this keeps up, I'll close the Comanche Chief. Now, what do you know about this feller who calls himself Van Avery?'

'What would we know about him?' countered Handsome.

'You probably wouldn't know anythin'. I got in touch with the Cattle Association, and asked them to recommend an investigator. Here is the answer.'

Steele handed the sheriff a telegram, which read—

GOOD LUCK

It was signed: 'James.'

'I think he means that he is sendin' or has sent the man he had in mind,' said Steele. 'Now, do you know anythin' about Van Avery?'

'Not a damn thing,' admitted the sheriff.

'Why was Van Avery shot this mornin'?'

'Reached for a gun,' said the sheriff. 'That's what Hawker said.'

'Miss Corey said he didn't have no gun,' added Handsome. 'And she said he never even reached for a gun. All he done was move his feet.'

'Wait a minute, Steele,' said the sheriff. 'Lemme git this straight. You think this Van Avery is a detective and that the higraders knew he was comin' and tried to murder him?'

'How does it look to you?'

41

Handsome chuckled softly.

'If he is, they didn't need to murder him. That jigger couldn't find his hat on a dance-hall floor.'

'Mebbe he wants to act thataway,' mused the sheriff.

'Yeah,' drawled Handsome. 'That's prob'ly why he ditched you at Red Hill last night.'

'What was that?' asked Steele.

'Didn't you notice Banty's skinned nose and chin? He done a high dive off a movin' train last night.'

The sheriff hastened to tell Steele about what really had happened, because Handsome's narrative might give a wrong impression.

'How did you happen to git that telegram?' queried Steele.

'It was sent to Harry Wall, the constable at Red Hill; but Harry wasn't in town and they gave it to me, bein' as I happened to be at the depot when the telegram came.'

'That ort to kinda prove that Van Avery ain't no detective,' said Handsome.

'Why not?' countered Steele. 'No pale-faced tenderfoot could ever stick up a Porcupine poker game and git away with it.'

'Not without a hell of a lot of luck.' Handsome laughed. 'Anyway, if this feller is a detective, he's shore disguised plenty.'

'Do you want to see Ken?' asked the sheriff.

Steele shook his head and got to his feet as another man came strolling in.

This man was tall and gaunt, with a huge, bony face, deep-set eyes and black hair. He was Rick Nelson, hardware merchant and proprietor of Nelson's Assay Office. Rick Nelson and Silver Steele had been friends for years. Milt Corey had hated both of them. At one time Corey had owned what was now the Comanche Chief mine. In fact, he had been the original discoverer; but adverse assay reports—reports made by Rick Nelson— had caused Corey to abandon the property, which was relocated by Silver Steele, subsequently becoming a rich producer.

If such had been the case, no one could point to the fact that Rick Nelson had ever profited by any such duplicity. However, it caused Milt Corey to make public statements as to the crooked methods of both Steele and Nelson, who ignored the statements; but it ended their friendship with Corey.

Corey was dead now, and Steele's son in jail facing a murder charge. Nelson was not wealthy by any means; but his little hardware store sup- plied the surrounding country, and he did a good business in his assaying, which he handled personally while a man named Dave Bush con- ducted the hardware business for him.

'Anything new on the holdup?' asked Nelson.

'Not yet,' said the sheriff. 'It wasn't much of a

holdup. There wasn't anythin' in the money-box, Rick.'

'That's what I heard. How's the feller who got shot?'

'He'll live, unless Doc Smedley experiments too much,' replied Handsome dryly.

'I don't like this holdup business,' said Nelson. 'Even if they didn't get anything this time, they might the next. That tenderfoot was mighty lucky he didn't get killed. Makes it kinda ticklish business for you to ship anything, don't it, Silver?'

'It would look thataway,' replied Steele grimly. 'But if I don't put a crimp in this higradin' deal I won't have anythin' to ship.'

'Why don't you hire a good detective?' asked Nelson.

'I suppose I'll have to do that, Rick. Can you recommend any?'

Nelson laughed huskily.

'No, I can't, Silver. Does anybody know when Corey is to be buried!'

'Prob'ly tomorrow,' answered the sheriff. 'Elene came home today.'

The assayer nodded.

'You goin'?' asked Handsome.

'Certainly. Corey had a damn poor opinion of me, but every man is entitled to his own opinions. You're goin', ain't you, Silver?'

'I'm no damn hypocrite!' snapped Steele. 'Of

course, I'm not goin'. With my son in jail for murderin' him, I'd look damn well at that funeral, wouldn't I?'

Nelson flushed beneath his leathery tan.

'Well, you said you'd disown him, if he—' began Nelson.

'What if I did?' Silver Steele got to his feet. 'A man might say anythin' when he's sore. You never had a son, Rick, so you don't know a damn thing about it. You can turn 'em down in fair weather, but if they're up against it, like my boy is—'

'Do you want to talk with him, Silver?' asked the sheriff softly.

'No, damn it, I don't! At least, not now.'

Silver Steele stepped outside and went up the street.

Rick Nelson laughed scornfully.

'After all his talkin'.'

'Well,' said the sheriff slowly, 'I think a damn sight more of Silver Steele than I ever did. I thought he was all guts and no heart.'

About fifteen minutes later, Hashknife and Sleepy stabled their horses. The sheriff met them as they were on their way to the hotel, and he recognized them as the two men who had been with Elene Corey when she got off the train at Red Hill.

It struck him that they might know something about Van Avery, so he stopped them.

Hashknife recognized him and smiled broadly.

'Didja ever get the man you was divin' after?' he asked.

'I wasn't divin' after him,' said the sheriff, grinning. 'That's my way of gettin' off trains.'

'Not very pretty, but it gits you all off,' remarked Sleepy.

'Got me all off. Jist git in from Red Hill?'

Hashknife nodded.

'Speakin' of that young man,' said the sheriff, 'he was shot on the way up here.'

'Shot?' queried Hashknife blankly.

'You happen to know anythin' about him?' asked the sheriff, after telling about the robbed stage and the shooting.

'He got on at Porcupine last night, and somebody shot at him through the coach window,' said Hashknife. 'He told us about how he stuck up a poker game and got his money back. I had a hunch them fellers might have wired ahead to stop him; so I told him to drop off the rear of the train at Red Hill.'

'That's how I missed him,' mused the sheriff. 'Well, it's all right. So that's all you know about him, eh?'

'Jist that much. What was the idea of them holdup men shootin' him down thataway?'

'*Quien sabe*?' The sheriff shrugged his shoulders. 'The girl said he didn't have any gun.'

'Lost it in his hurry to get on that train last

night,' said Sleepy. 'We advised him not to get another.'

'Good advice,' said the sheriff. 'You boys goin' to stay here awhile?'

'A few days, I reckon,' replied Hashknife. 'We're kinda lookin' over the country, tryin' to locate some good range land.'

'To buy?'

'No, I don't reckon we want to buy. Some of the bigger packing-houses are leasin' range, you know. They buy yearlin's in Mexico—buy 'em cheap—and throw 'em on leased ranges.'

'Yeah, I know they do.'

'How are things goin' around here?' asked Hashknife. 'Anythin' excitin' goin' on?'

'Not much,' admitted the sheriff. 'Pretty quiet country. Drop down to the office any time. We don't do much, but we talk plenty.'

It seemed as if everybody in the county came to Milt Corey's funeral. Hashknife and Sleepy saw Elene's sister, Mrs. Kenneth Steele, and her mother, a little wisp of a white-haired woman with pain-racked eyes. Mrs. Steele was younger than Elene, and she seemed to look defiantly at everyone.

Ed Ault, the gambler-proprietor of the Yucca Saloon and Gambling House, was there. He was tall, immaculate, with his small black mustache sharply outlined against his pale skin.

47

'Looks like a danged buzzard,' whispered Sleepy.

'Who?' queried Hashknife.

'That feller, Nelson, the assayer.'

Rick Nelson was not unlike a huge buzzard, standing there at the edge of the grave, dressed in a rusty black Prince Albert with a small black hat perched on his long head and his hands clasped behind him.

Sleepy whispered, 'And there's Young-Man-Proud-of-His-Name.'

It was Cornelius Van Avery, looking rather pale, a bandage around his head. Many glances were turned his way, but he did not seem to notice anybody except Elene Corey. Hashknife noticed that Ault was rather interested in Van Avery.

After the funeral was over, the Corey family rode away in their buggy at once. Van Avery joined Hashknife and Sleepy.

'You've been kinda cuttin' up since we seen you last,' said Hashknife.

Van Avery laughed nervously.

'But I did not do a thing. That man with the cloth over his face said something to me, and the next thing I knew I was there alone in the road.'

'Did they really take two thousand dollars from your pocket?' asked Sleepy, who was a bit skeptical about the robbery.

'Yes, they did; but they overlooked five hundred dollars.'

'Kinda looks as though your Porcupine friends cut in and took back their winnin's,' observed Sleepy.

'That is worth considering,' agreed Van Avery. 'But how would they know I got off at Red Hill, and how would they know I was on that stage?'

'It's only about ten miles,' replied Hashknife. 'They might have ridden over, found you was at the hotel, watched you git on the stage, and then cut in ahead of you—unless you can figure out a better reason for somebody shootin' you down thataway.'

'I really can't,' admitted Van Avery.

'Are you goin' over there and make 'em give it back?' asked Sleepy.

'I'm not exactly sure just what to do. There really should be an example made of men who shoot other men, don't you think?'

Hashknife inhaled deeply on his cigarette and looked keenly at Van Avery.

'Jist what is your business, Van Avery?' he asked.

'Why, I really haven't any business,' replied the young man frankly. 'You see, my father wanted me to stay in Pittsburgh after I tried to finish college. Oh, I did try hard. They even sent me to Stanford, over on the Pacific Coast. I tried real hard, but I—I did not seem to grasp things as I should. Then my mother died.'

A note of sadness crept into his voice, and he looked away for a moment.

'Mother was fine. Not that Dad isn't great, too, but he doesn't understand a fellow. Mother left me some money. Not a great deal, but—well, enough—and I wanted to do things, you see. I wanted to get away from the city. And'—Van Avery smiled broadly and spread his hands—'here I am.'

'Yeah, here you are,' agreed Hashknife. 'Pardner, you need a keeper.'

'Why?'

'Well, you've lost two thousand dollars already.'

'Lost it twice,' corrected Van Avery. 'Do you believe in third times?'

'Not with that money.' Hashknife grinned. 'You'll never see that money again.'

'Will you tell your dad about it?' asked Sleepy.

'I should say not! Why, if Dad knew I had been shot and robbed he would have a fit. He has always lived in the city. You really have to live down here in Arizona to appreciate getting shot, don't you think?'

Hashknife choked over some tobacco smoke.

'Gittin' shot down here don't mean nothin',' said Sleepy.

'I know it. Doctor Smedley seemed rather disappointed over my wound. I thought it was bad enough; but he said mine wasn't hardly worth

50

wasting thread on. I wonder where I can buy me another gun.'

'At the hardware store,' replied Hashknife.

'Thank you; I shall get one today.'

'Figgerin' on gunnin' somebody?' asked Hashknife curiously.

'No one in particular; I merely thought I should like to have one.' And Van Avery went on toward Rick Nelson's store.

'Can you imagine a jigger like that?' asked Sleepy.

Hashknife snapped his cigarette into the dusty street as they walked toward the sheriff's office. Handsome was in the doorway and grinned a welcome. He had seen them talking with Van Avery and he wondered what their opinion of Van Avery might be.

'If he lives long enough he may learn somethin',' said Hashknife.

'He'd have to live a long time then,' retorted Sleepy.

Handsome sprawled in his chair.

'That's my idea, too,' he said, 'but somebody else thinks different.'

'That so?' queried Hashknife. 'Some fortune-teller?'

'Some fortune-loser,' laughed Handsome. 'You see, Silver Steele, who owns the Comanche Chief mine, claims that higraders have been hookin' him out of a lot of money. Quite a while ago there was a prospector here named Jack Cherry. He was around here quite a spell, and all to once he's found at the bottom of a twelve-foot prospect hole, deader 'n hell, along with half a quart of whiskey.

'We jist found out that his right name was Payzant, and he was a detective hired by Steele; and Steele says he never drank. Steele says he got in touch with the Cattlemen's Association and asked them to send him the best man they knowed anythin' about. He's got a telegram which jist says "Good luck," which he figgers means they've got the right man for the job. And Steele thinks this here rib-shot tenderfoot is that detective.'

'Well, sir, he might be!' exclaimed Hashknife seriously. 'You know, them detectives do queer things, Handsome.'

Sleepy coughed and went to the door to get a breath of air. He had tears in his eyes as he turned to come back. But at that moment they heard what seemed to be the muffled report of a gun. As Hashknife and Handsome got to their feet, they heard four more shots in rapid succession.

The three men ran out to the sidewalk, just in time to see Cornelius Van Avery back out of the hardware store doorway. He stopped in the middle of the sidewalk as if undecided, saw the three men in front of the office and came down toward them.

As he started, Dave Bush, who ran the store for Nelson, sprang out to the middle of the sidewalk and yelled at Van Avery:

'You come back here, you damn fool!'

Van Avery stopped and looked back. He dusted the palms of his hands on his hips and shook his head.

'I certainly shall not,' he said firmly.

Rick Nelson came from his office and talked with Bush, who was gesticulating wildly, but speaking in a normal tone. Van Avery came to the front of the sheriff's office, his expression very serious. He looked back at Nelson and Bush.

'Why should I go back?' asked Van Avery. 'Am I to blame in any way?'

'Who was doin' all that shootin'?' asked Handsome.

'I was,' replied Van Avery casually.

'You was? What in hell was you shootin' at?'

'Nothing in particular.'

'You didn't hit anybody, didja?' asked Sleepy.

Van Avery shook his head, keeping an eye on Bush and Nelson, who were coming toward him. Several others, who had heard the shooting, were also on their way to find out what had happened.

Dave Bush was an anemic-looking man of about forty, bony of face, and with a very prominent pair of ears.

'Well, what happened, anyway?' growled Handsome.

'This feller,' said Bush, pointing at Van Avery, 'shot up the store. I tell you, he didn't miss my ear an inch!'

'Would be kinda hard to miss,' said Handsome dryly as he turned to Van Avery. 'Why didja shoot up the store?'

'That gun would not stop going off,' replied Van Avery.

'Well, you poor fool!' snapped Bush. 'I told you—'

'You tell it, young man,' interrupted Handsome. 'Mr. Bush is kinda excited over almost losin' a ear.'

Van Avery took a deep breath and smiled weakly.

'Well, it was like this: I went in there to purchase a gun. This man said he had the sort of gun I needed, and he showed me a gun. I took the gun, but it was rather strange; so I—'

'What kind of a gun was it, Bush?' asked the deputy.

'A Colt .45 automatic,' growled Bush.

'I know the gun,' grunted Handsome. 'You couldn't sell it to a man, so you tried to shove it off on this—' pointing at Van Avery.

'It's a damn good gun,' insisted Bush.

'There is something wrong with it,' said Van Avery.

'You don't know anything about a gun, that's your trouble.'

'Well, what's to be done about it?' asked Handsome. 'Nobody hurt. You can't expect the young man to buy it, can you?'

'No, I don't,' grunted Bush. 'He hadn't ought to have a gun—he's dangerous.'

'I'm not dangerous,' retorted Van Avery, 'but that gun you loaded for me is certainly dangerous. It wouldn't stop shooting.'

'I found that out,' replied Bush. 'But you didn't need to throw it through that back window.'

'The window,' said Van Avery, 'was merely incidental; I just threw it, and the window happened to be there.'

Nelson laughed at Van Avery's explanation, then turned to Bush.

'If the young man feels the need of a gun, sell him a good one. But take my advice and send that automatic to a gunsmith.'

'All right,' replied Bush ungraciously. 'But if I sell him a gun, he'll have to load it outside the store. I'm all jumpy yet.'

'I'll sell it to him,' Nelson said, and Van Avery followed him back to the store.

'Detective!' snorted Handsome. 'Who ever heard of a detective who couldn't handle a gun.'

'Mebbe he's still actin',' Sleepy put in. 'You know, he missed that feller's ear.'

'Yeah, he did.'

'Not bad shootin', after seein' them ears,' said Hashknife dryly. 'You were talkin' about men stealin' ore from the Comanche Chief. How do they handle it?'

'You mean, how do they steal it?'

'No; how do they get rid of it? You can't dig coined gold right out of the ground, you know. It has to be minted.'

'Hell, I know that. I suppose that's why Steele hired a detective—to find out them things.'

'Ain't you and the sheriff been workin' on it any?'

Handsome laughed at the idea.

'I'm afraid we wouldn't be much help,' he confessed.

'What about the murder of Corey?'

'Oh, that! We've got the boy who pulled that deal.'

'What did he do with the money he stole?'

'Nobody knows but him, and he won't tell. He's Steele's son, and he married Milt Corey's daughter. You seen her at the funeral. She's an awful nice girl, and I shore feel sorry for her. Feel sorry for the old lady too. She's worked mighty hard. You see, the bank won't extend their mortgage no more, and they was a-goin' to foreclose; but Ed Ault loaned the old man ten thousand on a note. That was the ten thousand that Ken Steele got away with, after he popped the old man. Now the Coreys owe Ault ten thousand and the bank ten thousand. That's a hell of a lot of money; more than the Corey ranch is worth.'

'What kind of a feller is Ault?' asked Sleepy.

'I'll tell you what kind of a feller he is. Ault was crazy over Gladys Corey, but Ken beat him out of her. Then Ault turns right around and lends her father ten thousand dollars on a note. Ault ain't no dog in the manger, y'betcha. No, he's all right. Runs his games on the square and behaves himself.'

'It seems that 'most everybody liked Milt Corey,' said Hashknife.

'Why not? He was salt of the earth, Old Milt was. He wasn't awful pleased over Gladys marryin' Ken, but he never squawked; and when Ken's father told him to git to hell off the place, Corey gave him a job punchin' cows.'

'Ken Steele was kinda in debt himself, wasn't he?'

'Yeah. Got drunk a couple of times and shore run in debt. Ken can't play poker worth a darn. I reckon he owed Ault over a thousand dollars. Ault let him run in debt, thinkin' Ken's father would pay the bill, but Silver told Ault to go to hell. Ken had a house here in town, and a couple horses and a few cows; so Ault attached everythin' he owned after Ken was arrested.'

'Pretty tough deal on the Corey family,' observed Hashknife.

He and Sleepy wandered up to a Chinese restaurant, where they ordered a meal.

'Well, we know what we was sent here to do,'

said Sleepy. 'Personally, I ain't lost no higraders and if you take my advice, you'd wire the Cattlemen's Association that we had resigned and was headin' for a high hill again.'

CHAPTER III
ED AULT GOES VISITING

Corey's Diamond C brand was one of the old marks in that part of the country. His ranch was located three miles east of Painted Wells, a rather picturesque old huddle of adobe buildings under some spreading sycamores.

Milt Corey had never aspired to be a big cattle-raiser, but was content to live along, loving his family and home. Two or three droughts in succession and low prices for beef and hides had depleted his scanty capital, as it had that of many cattlemen in that country.

The banks would lend no more money on that sort of security. Milt Corey had secured the ten-thousand-dollar mortgage when the market was in good shape, but bad luck had prevented him from paying off any of the principal. Now there was not only the mortgage due, but the note held by Ed Ault for the same amount, due in less than six months. On the day following the funeral, Ed Ault rode out to the Corey ranch. Ault was no philanthropist; he was a cold-blooded gambler. He rode into the shady patio, watered his horse at the well and tied it to an iron ring in the patio wall.

Mrs. Corey came out on the rear veranda as

Ault turned. She was a frail little woman, dressed in rusty black. He came up and leaned against the rail.

'Won't you come up and sit down?' she asked.

'Thank you,' replied Ault gravely. 'I wasn't sure if I'd be welcome out here.'

'There has always been a welcome for anybody here, Mr. Ault.'

'I know it, Mrs. Corey. You folks have had hard luck—mighty hard—and I wanted to tell you not to worry about that note.'

'I know you mean well, Mr. Ault,' said the old lady slowly. 'The bank foreclosed today. We have one year to redeem the mortgage, but I don't see how it can be done. If we can't, I suppose the bank will sell the property, take their money, and pay you what is left.'

Ault nodded thoughtfully.

'Yes, I reckon that's what they'll do.'

'One more year,' said the old lady softly. 'It has been home for a good many years. We've worked hard, and we've been good to everybody. I suppose it is the Lord's will, but it is hard to understand.'

'Has Ken got a lawyer yet, Mrs. Corey?'

'Poor Ken. No, he hasn't.'

Ault looked at her queerly.

'Can you feel sorry for Ken?'

The old lady lifted her head and looked at him wearily.

'Why, of course. We do not believe Ken did it.'
The gambler smiled.

'I hope he can prove that to a jury, Mrs. Corey.'

'I feel sure he can. Poor Glad, it was a terrible shock to her.'

'Naturally. She's a great girl. You knew how I felt about her. Well, I haven't changed a bit. That attachment I took on Ken's stuff don't mean a thing. I didn't know who else he owed money to; so I figured I'd protect Gladys by putting on the first attachment. When this deal is over, I'll turn everything back to her, don't you see?'

'Why should you? It was an honest debt, wasn't it?'

'Certainly it was an honest debt, but it doesn't mean much to me. I've made plenty of money— enough for me. Some of these days I'll sell out and live easy the rest of my life. I'm young yet.'

'Yes, you have been successful,' said Mrs. Corey.

Elene came out on the veranda, and Ault got quickly to his feet.

'I've wanted to see you and welcome you back,' he said rapidly. 'How did you like the city?'

Elene shook her head slowly.

'I like Arizona,' she said softly.

'And you belong here,' he said quickly. 'Arizona for Arizonians, eh? The city is all right for city folks, but Arizona is for people who really want to live. City folks never—'

'For goodness' sake!' exclaimed Mrs. Corey.

Cornelius Van Avery had stopped inside the patio gate. He was hatless, his shirt was torn in a dozen places, and his face scratched. He limped painfully. He was wearing an ornate pair of chaps, a huge pair of Mexican spurs on his fancy boots. His holster flapped empty at his thigh.

Elene got quickly to her feet and went to the top of the steps. Van Avery saw her, reached for the hat he did not have on, and came up to the bottom step, grimacing painfully.

'So this is your home,' he said. 'Goodness, what a time I've had!'

'Come up and sit down,' begged Elene. 'Mother, this is Mr. Van Avery.'

'Mrs. Corey, the pleasure is mine, I assure you.'

'Mr. Van Avery, this is Mr. Ault.'

'Oh, yes.' Van Avery smiled. 'Mr. Ault, how do you do.'

'All right,' grunted Ault.

'That is fine. I wish I was.'

'Didn't you bring your horse?' queried Ault with a trace of sarcasm.

Van Avery attempted to flex his toes inside his boots and grimaced from the pain.

'That horse,' he said seriously, 'had ideas of his own. The sheriff explained to me just how to get out here; but I suppose he should have let the horse in on the secret.'

'Did you fall off?' asked Ault.

'I suppose something like that happened. The real reason is locked in the brain of that yellow horse. You see, he stopped and turned around, intending, no doubt, to return home.'

Van Avery turned one heel a trifle and glanced at the wicked-looking spur.

'The man who sold me those spurs said they would be great to ride a bronc with. I don't know. Perhaps that wasn't a bronc. I jabbed him just once, and my next jab was in a thorn-bush. Since then I've been strolling around looking for this place.'

'It's very lucky you wasn't hurt,' said Mrs. Corey. 'I'll bet your feet are blistered.'

'Mrs. Corey,' said Van Avery seriously, 'I'd amend that to say that I have very little feet on my blister. If there are any unblistered spots on my feet, I don't know where they are.'

'Yeah, and if you take off them boots, you won't be able to get 'em on again, I'll bet,' said Ault. 'I don't know why you tenderfeet ever come out to a man's country. You never listen to any advice; just go blind.'

'I beg your pardon,' said Van Avery stiffly. 'I have no recollection of you or anybody else giving me advice. The only advice I have received was from a man named Hashknife Hartley. He advised me not to carry a gun; but I—darn it, that one is gone now! I suppose it is still in that thorn-bush.'

'Well, you are going to have those feet taken care of right here and now,' declared Mrs. Corey rising. 'Elene, you get that foot-tub while I get the cotton and the rest of the stuff.'

'I'll warn you now,' said Ault, 'you'll never be able to get your boots on again until your feet heal. You take my horse and ride him back to town, and tell the stableman to bring it back for me.'

'He's not going back to town,' declared Mrs. Corey. 'Who does he know in town who can fix his feet? You sit down, young man.'

Van Avery laughed as he thanked Mrs. Corey.

'Much obliged to you, too, Mr. Ault; but I'm not riding so well today. When you go back, I wish you would tell the stableman about that yellow horse. It is very likely at home by this time.'

Ault waited to say good-bye to Elene and her mother before he rode away. Elene brought a bootjack, and they managed to get the boots off Van Avery's swollen feet.

'I feel like a perfect fool,' complained Van Avery. 'Why should you ladies bother with me?'

'You sit still,' ordered Mrs. Corey. 'My goodness, if you went back to town with those feet! You must have walked miles. Never do that in high-heeled boots.'

'What would a cowboy have done?' he asked.

Mrs. Corey laughed pleasantly.

'Very few cowboys lose their horses; and they are such poor walkers that they'd prob'ly set down and starve to death. Mr. Van Avery, this is my daughter, Mrs. Steele.'

Van Avery looked up to see Mrs. Steele. Elene came past her with the little tub of water.

'Gladys, this is the young man I told you about,' she said.

'I'm mighty glad to meet you, Mrs. Steele,' said Van Avery, 'but I'm also mighty ashamed to have all these blisters.'

'Don't mind the blisters,' said Mrs. Steele, sitting down on the top step. 'If we had nothing worse than a few blisters—'

'That's right.' Van Avery nodded seriously. 'I talked with Hashknife Hartley this morning about you folks. You remember him, Miss Corey—the tall cowboy on the train?'

'Yes, I remember him. But why should he be interested in us?'

'Oh, I suppose it is because there is so much talk about you. He is looking over the range land for some packing company, I believe.'

Mrs. Corey finished doctoring Van Avery's feet, and Elene brought him an old pair of moccasins to wear. He thanked her gravely. He asked how he could get back to Painted Wells.

'You will stay right here,' declared the old lady. 'No use going back to town. What would you do—sit in a stuffy hotel room until your feet heal?'

'But I couldn't impose upon you folks; really I couldn't, Mrs. Corey.'

'You are not imposing on us,' said Mrs. Corey. 'You sit right here on the porch and rest. It will be good for all of us to have someone to talk with.'

'I'm not much to talk with,' Van Avery said. 'Really, I'm dumb. No, I mean it. Several very learned professors have told me the same thing; a number of well-known lawyers have offered to prove that I am dumb, and my own father has hinted the same thing.'

'And now you are willing to admit it,' said Mrs. Steele.

'No question about it. But the sensation isn't so terrible. Not having any natural sense, everything I do is in the nature of a discovery. Now, take that horse, for instance. No, I'd rather not. The subject is painful.'

Elene laughed as she removed the tub.

'You haven't been shot at lately, have you?' she asked.

'Not since the doctor fixed me up. I remarked that to Hashknife Hartley today, and he told me not to get impatient.'

'That Mr. Hartley appears to be a capable sort of a man,' remarked Elene.

'He really does, doesn't he? His eyes are so clear and he talks softly. I like Sleepy Stevens, too, but he seems to be laughing at me all the time. He wants me to change my name. My full name is Cornelius Shelton Van Avery. Sleepy said I ought to—let me see, what was the word he used? Oh, yes, dehorn. He said to dehorn both front and back, and make it Blondy Van.'

'Your hair is blond,' teased Elene. 'You could hardly escape a nickname in this country.'

'I suppose not; but I don't mind. Now, I've talked too much about myself. That's a bad habit of mine. Gee, my feet feel fine!'

'Was it true that those men robbed you of two thousand dollars?' asked Elene.

'Yes, it was true. At least, two thousand was missing. They overlooked five hundred, luckily for me. Hashknife thinks that those men came over from Porcupine, thinking perhaps I got off the train at Red Hill, saw me get on the stage and later robbed me.'

Elene nodded.

'That would account for the fact that they shot you.'

'That was a terrible thing to do,' said Mrs. Corey. 'Elene was sure you were dead. She said they deliberately shot you down.'

The talk gradually drifted around to their own troubles, and Van Avery heard a first-hand account of it all. In spite of the evidence against him, none of them believed Ken Steele had shot Milt Corey.

'Ken loved Dad,' said Gladys miserably. 'He'd

have done anything for him; and they say he did this.'

'Ed Ault was here today, Gladys,' said Mrs. Corey.

'I know he was, and that was why I didn't come out.'

'He said he attached Ken's property to protect you.'

'How in the world would that help Glad?' demanded Elene.

'He explained that he didn't know how many other debts Ken had; so he protected her with the first attachment. He said she could have the property any time she wanted it.'

'In plain English, he wants to make Gladys a present of Ken's gambling debts, all nicely cancelled,' said Elene. 'Why?'

'Never look a gift horse in the mouth,' said Gladys.

'I'd look that one in the mouth,' declared Elene firmly.

'Would you? It doesn't seem to me that we can pick and choose, Elene.'

'Listen, honey.' Elene went over and put an arm around Mrs. Steele's shoulders. 'Ken hasn't been convicted yet. When he is, it will be plenty time for Ed Ault to be offering you presents.'

'You haven't any right to say that,' flared Mrs. Steele, getting to her feet quickly. 'You act as though I had forgotten Ken.'

'Oh, I'm sorry,' said Elene, 'but you know I never liked Ed Ault.'

'Because he's a gambler,' retorted Mrs. Steele. 'Oh, I'm not going to defend Ed Ault. He's nothing to me and never was. If I cared for him in any way, I'd have come out and spoken to him, wouldn't I? I suppose I should hate him for letting Ken run up those gambling debts. But I know they were honest debts, because Ed Ault is an honest gambler.'

Mrs. Steele walked into the house, rather defiantly. Mrs. Corey shook her head sadly.

'Well, I'm not alone,' said Van Avery thoughtfully.

'What do you mean?' asked Elene curiously.

'I thought I was the only person in the state to make dumb statements,' he said seriously. 'Honest gambler!'

'Do you know where your detective is now?' asked Banty Brayton, digging at the bowl of his old pipe, which seemed to be eternally plugged up.

'I didn't say he was my detective,' denied Silver Steele. 'I just wondered if he was.'

'Uh-huh. Damned pipe! I wish I could git used to smokin' cigarettes. Well, he hired a horse and started out to the Corey ranch yesterday, but the horse bucked him off in a manzanita, and he had to walk halfway around the world to find the ranch. Didn't have brains enough to foller a road.

Landed at the ranch with his heels all blistered; and he's still out there waitin' for 'em to heal.'

'He'd make a good sheriff,' observed Handsome. 'Lost his gun.'

Steele laughed shortly.

'I reckon I was mistaken about who he is. What do you know about these two strange cowboys?'

'Hartley and Stevens?' asked Handsome.

'Yeah. What are they doin' here?'

'Oh, they're workin' for some Eastern packin' outfit, lookin' over new range for their feeders. Jist a couple cowboys, gittin' along.'

'How are things up at the mine?' asked the sheriff.

'Better. I clamped down hard. Offered a thousand dollars reward to any miner who could give me information on who was stealin' higrade ore, and I offered five thousand to anyone who could show me how the higraders got rid of their ore.'

'I reckon I'll quit bein' a officer and start detectin',' said Handsome.

'You can start right here,' said Steele quickly.

'What do you mean?'

'I'll give you five thousand to prove that Ken never killed Milt Corey.'

'Steele, I'd do that for nuthin', if I was able.'

'I know you would. How is Ken?'

'Eatin' three times a day. His wife and her sister came in last evenin' to see him. Want to go in and talk with him?'

Steele shook his head.

'Ken and I parted with some hot words. We were both wrong, and we're both bull-headed. I'm goin' to hire the best criminal lawyer I can find.'

'I wonder what Ken done with that ten thousand dollars,' said the sheriff.

'You might ask him,' suggested Handsome. 'I did.'

'What did he say?'

'Repeatin' profanity allus hurts my tonsils.'

'As a matter of fact, there's only Ken's gun as evidence against him,' stated Steele.

'That's all.' The sheriff nodded. 'But that's a-plenty. It's all wrapped up and locked in the old safe.'

The safe in question was a huge old relic, without a combination.

'I'd hate to use a safe like that,' said Steele.

'If there was ever anythin' valuable in it, so would I,' joked the sheriff.

Hashknife and Sleepy came in; and the sheriff introduced them to Steele. Sleepy wanted to play a game of pool, so Handsome offered to play him, if 'spotted' enough to allow him a big advantage. They went away arguing the point, and in a few minutes Steele departed.

The sheriff told Hashknife of the different rewards Steele had offered.

'Why don't he hire a good detective?' asked Hashknife.

71

'He thinks he has.' The sheriff chuckled.

'Van Avery?'

'You heard about Van Avery, didn't you?'

'I heard Ault tell what happened to him. Still out there?'

'I suppose he is.'

Hashknife rolled a smoke and sprawled in his chair.

'Was Milt Corey ever interested in minin'?' he asked.

'You've heard about him givin' up the Comanche Chief?'

'Yeah, but I mean later.'

'No. Oh, yes, he was once.' The sheriff explained: 'You see, Rick Nelson found some likely lookin' stuff jist a short distance from Corey's north line fence and sunk a short shaft. Corey found out about it, and located several claims on his own land on his side of the fence. You see, that stopped Nelson from locatin' on Corey's land.'

'Could he have done that?'

'Shore, if he could prove it was more valuable for minerals than for grazin'.'

'That's right. You see, I'm a cowpuncher, not a miner. Then what happened?'

'Nelson quit—said it was jist a surface showin'. That was two years ago. Nelson's claim lapsed, 'cause he never done his assessment work last year. But Corey did. Corey wasn't no judge of ore, but he hated and suspected Nelson; so he done his assessment work to keep Nelson from ever grabbin' that land.'

'What did Nelson think about it?'

'Well, it amused Nelson. He said he'd keep Corey doin' assessment work as long as he lived. It was Nelson's idea of a good joke. I saw the stuff Nelson took out. It assayed a little gold at the surface, but the vein was thin as a hay-fever whisper, and played out complete. Say, I forgot to tell you—it was that prospect hole where that feller Payzant was killed.'

'Yeah?' Hashknife inhaled deeply and blew a thin stream of smoke toward the dingy ceiling.

'Payzant was supposed to be a prospector, and he was workin' on a little lead about a mile east of that prospect hole.'

'Who found him?' asked Hashknife.

'Couple cowboys from Steele's outfit. Goin' past, they saw a hat on the edge of the hole; so they got off and took a look.'

'You say it's on Corey's north line fence, eh?'

'Shore. You ain't goin' in for prospectin', are you, Hartley?'

'Pshaw, I wouldn't know one ore from another. All I know is cows.'

'That's me. Ore ain't nothin' but rock to me.'

'What about the prospect Payzant was workin' on?' asked Hashknife.

'Didn't amount to anythin'. Nelson said he

didn't have any kind of a showin'. I jist wonder if Steele was right about Payzant. I mean about him not drinkin'. He looked as though he had fell in on his head, and there was a whiskey bottle, part full, beside him.'

'How deep was the hole?'

'Mebbe fifteen feet deep.'

'Solid rock bottom?'

'Shore.'

'Didn't it strike you that the bottle must have been tough to stand a fall like that?'

'It does now; we never paid no attention at the time. Payzant must have been dead several days. It shore wasn't a nice job—takin' him out.'

'Bury him here?'

'Yeah. The boys chipped in and gave him a decent burial.'

Hashknife wandered up town and found Silver Steele at a general store. Hashknife bought some tobacco, and a little later joined Steele at the hitch-rack, where Steele was loading some stuff in a buckboard.

'The sheriff was telling me a few things about local happenin's,' said Hashknife, 'and he mentioned a detective named Payzant. I used to know a cowpuncher of that name, and I wondered if he had turned detective. It ain't a common name.'

'Might be the same man,' said Steele. 'This man was of medium size, dark hair—'

'Different man,' interrupted Hashknife. 'The

74

one I knew was as tall as I am. The sheriff was tellin' me somethin' of how Payzant met his death, and that he didn't know until lately that Payzant was a detective.'

'That's right,' agreed the big mine-owner. 'I was payin' a detective agency to furnish me a first-class man. They warned me that I would never know who he was until the case was closed. I never suspected this man, who said his name was Jack Cherry. Even after his body was found and buried, I never suspected who he was. That was how he happened to be buried here. It was quite a long time later that a letter came to him, sent in care of me, and the postmaster gave it to me. You see, we never knew where he came from; so I opened this letter, hopin' it would be from some relative, and it was from the detective agency, askin' why he didn't report to them.'

'Do you think he was murdered?' asked Hashknife.

'I do. No one ever saw him take a drink, and I believe the bottle was planted there to give the impression he was drunk and fell into the hole.'

'The bottle wasn't busted, and the sheriff says the hole was fifteen feet deep.' Hashknife affirmed.

'I never thought of that, but it's true.'

'This ore-stealin' proposition is plumb new to me,' said Hashknife. 'I can savvy 'em stealin' rich ore; but I'll be danged if I can see how

75

they get the gold out of it and dispose of it.'

'That's the problem, Hartley. You show me how it is done, and I'll give you a check for five thousand cold dollars. And here's another chance to make a stake: Find out that my son didn't kill Milt Corey, and I'll give you another five thousand.'

Hashknife laughed and shook his head.

'I'm no detective, Mr. Steele.'

'That's right. Well, come out and see us, Hartley. Come out to the ranch or out to the mine. You're always welcome.'

'Thank you kindly.' Hashknife nodded.

Steele drove away.

Hashknife sauntered back along the street to Nelson's hardware store, where he found Dave Bush alone behind the counter.

'Seen anythin' of the darn gun-shootin' tender-foot?' asked Bush, taking a seat on the counter.

'He's out at Corey's place, I reckon,' replied Hashknife.

'I hope he stays there. That jigger is positively dangerous.'

'Next time don't sell a faulty automatic,' advised Hashknife.

'Well, I didn't know it wouldn't stay cocked.' Bush laughed. 'I was takin' chances, I guess. He bought a Colt .45 revolver from Rick. Damn fool will probably shoot himself with it.'

'I wonder if he's as dumb as he acts.'

'I'm wonderin' the same thing,' replied Bush seriously. 'Wasn't he mixed up in some sort of a shootin' deal in Porcupine?'

'I reckon he was. What kind of a place is Porcupine?'

'Saloon and a post-office.'

'No stores?'

'No. Started in as a minin' town, but failed fast. Nothin' much over there except the X8X cattle outfit, Steve McCord's place.'

'Where do they trade—over here?'

'Yeah. We get most of the trade. Steve and Rick are old friends, and we fill most of their orders. Sometimes they come over after it, and other times we ship it down on a train. Don't amount to much. More of an accommodation than anythin' else.'

'No mines workin' now?'

'No, you can't say there is. Steve owns a hole in the ground and a broken-down stamp mill. Used to be the Hellbender Minin' Company. I reckon Steve inherited it or won it in a poker game. They did take out some gold at one time, but not any more. The last time I saw Steve, he was talkin' about puttin' a couple men to work, kinda pesticatin' around, lookin' for the lost vein.'

'I hear he runs sort of a forked outfit,' said Hashknife.

'Well, I suppose they are. You've got to hold your own in a country like this. Steve's only got three men, besides himself and the cook. You ought to meet Steve; he's the kind you'd like to find at the wagon.'

Hashknife smiled.

'You've punched cows yourself, eh?'

'Oh, yeah, a little. What made you think that?'

'Mentionin' meetin' him at the wagon,' replied Hashknife. 'What do you think of this case against young Steele?'

'Pretty bad for him, it looks to me. In the first place, Ken needed money pretty bad. That would prob'ly cover any of us; but findin' his gun near the body, one empty shell and blood on the gun— you see, the old man was beat over the head.'

'Ken offer any alibi?'

'Said he was innocent and then shut up like a clam.'

A customer came in, and Hashknife sauntered outside. For lack of something better to do, he wandered up to the stage depot, where the stage was loading for the trip down to Red Hill. He sat down on an old bench in front of the office, and in a few minutes Ed Ault and one of his men came over to the stage. Ault was carrying a suitcase and was apparently dressed for traveling.

They stopped near Hashknife, waiting for the loading to finish, and Ault gave his companion detailed orders on running the business during his absence. Ault nodded to Hashknife.

'Takin' a vacation?' asked Hashknife.

'Going to Phoenix for a few days,' replied Ault. 'Have to get away once in a while to keep from growin' rusty.'

Ault climbed aboard, and the stage was on its dusty way to Red Hill again. Hashknife watched it disappear, then sauntered back down the street. Hashknife did not like Painted Wells; and he did not like the sort of work expected of him. Mining stuff was out of his line, and, except for the little old white-haired Mrs. Corey, he would have wired the Association to select another man for the job, and have gone riding toward the hills again.

Hashknife was queerly sentimental. He did not know Mrs. Corey. He had merely seen her at the funeral. Yet he could not forget that expression of dumb misery on her wrinkled old face as she stood there trying to realize that her lifetime partner was gone, her home to be taken away from her, and her daughter's husband facing a murder charge.

'Old folks hadn't ought to suffer,' he told himself. 'They ain't got nothin' to look forward to—no chance to build up again. I'd always hate myself if I went away and didn't help her. There's one crooked deal been pulled on that outfit, and I've got to see if I've got brains enough to straighten it out. But, Lord, I don't know where to start.'

CHAPTER IV
HIGRADERS

At eight o'clock that evening, Sleepy and Handsome were in a small poker game at the Yucca Saloon, and Hashknife was sitting with the sheriff in front of his office, when a team and light wagon came rattling down the street and drew up at the little hitch-rack in front of the sheriff's office.

Elene Corey was driving the team, and with her were Mrs. Corey, Mrs. Steele, and Cornelius Van Avery. Both Hashknife and the sheriff realized that this was unusual; but none of the visitors made any explanation until they were inside the office where the others were able to see Van Avery. He had a cut lip; two lower front teeth were missing, and his light-colored shirt seemed to be a smear of gore.

'I'm rather a thight,' he said, lisping through the space where he had lost the two teeth.

The three women seemed frightened and nervous, although none of them had been injured.

'We just had to come in,' explained Elene nervously. 'Mr. Van Avery insisted that he—he must get away from there, and—'

'Jist what in the world happened to you?' queried Hashknife.

Van Avery essayed a weak grin.

'Someone shot through the window!' said Mrs. Corey.

'Shot through the window!' ejaculated the sheriff. 'Who did, Mrs. Corey?'

The little old lady shook her head.

'We were eating dinner, and—'

'Supper,' corrected Mrs. Steele.

'Oh, yeth. I was eating thoup, and thomebody—Mith Corey, will you tell it, pleath.'

Elene suppressed a nervous laugh.

'That lisp may sound funny, but it must be painful to have two perfectly good teeth knocked out by a saltshaker.'

'Well, suppose we git down to exactly what happened,' suggested the sheriff.

'Someone fired a shot through the window,' said Mrs. Corey. 'The bullet apparently struck a saltcellar, and the saltcellar struck Blondy—Mr. Van Avery—in the mouth.'

'That'th all right.' Van Avery grinned. 'Call me Blondy. You thee'—turning to the sheriff—'I'm thure thomebody was thootin' at me, and I—I don't with anybody elth to get hurt. That'th why I inthithted on coming back to town tonight.'

'And we were afraid to stay out there,' added Elene. 'That is the whole story.'

The sheriff shook his head wonderingly as he looked at the disheveled Van Avery.

'Boy, I don't savvy your luck. That's the third

time somebody has tried to kill you. Don'tcha know you're settin' a record for Arizona?'

'I'm not interethted in recordth.'

'I don't blame you ladies for bein' scared,' said Hashknife. 'It was plenty nervy of you to even stop to hitch up a team. I don't reckon I'd have stopped to bother with a horse. Are you goin' to stay here in town tonight?'

'We never thought just what we might do,' confessed the white-haired lady. 'We would be afraid to go back.'

'I wouldn't go back there alone for a million dollars,' declared Mrs. Steele.

Hashknife and the sheriff looked at each other curiously.

'I don't believe we'd care to stay at the hotel,' said Elene.

'I'll tell you what,' suggested Hashknife. 'I'll go git my pardner, and we'll go out with you—if you'd like to have us. I'm sure there is no danger out there now.'

'Would you do that?' asked Elene eagerly.

'Be ready in five minutes. I'll drive your team and let Sleepy take our horses. Blondy, you better hunt up Doc Smedley and have him fix up your lip. He can't do much for the teeth, I'm afraid.'

'I gueth not,' lisped Van Avery. 'I think I thwallowed 'em.'

The trip back to the ranch was uneventful. The women had not stopped to clean up the wreck of their interrupted supper. There was the smashed window, scattered dishes, the battered metal saltcellar which had struck Van Avery's teeth. Hashknife found the bullet embedded in the wall.

After an investigation, Hashknife deduced that the bullet had been fired at Van Avery, who sat at the end of the table; but the aim had been low and the bullet had struck the bowl of a heavy soup spoon about three feet from Van Avery. Apparently the bullet had ricocheted, missing Van Avery by several inches.

The bullet was considerably battered, but Hashknife decided that it was a .45-70 caliber. An investigation outside the house satisfied Hashknife that the shooter had been on horseback, as there were no fences or buildings near, and the angle showed conclusively that the bullet had been fired on a downward slant.

All of which was little satisfaction to the three women; but Hashknife finally persuaded them that it was merely another attempt upon the life of Van Avery, and not an attack on them.

The sheriff came out there early in the morning, but there was nothing for him to investigate. Near a gate just north of the house Hashknife found an empty .45-70 shell which showed no stains of weather.

'The man who fired that shot was on horseback,' said Hashknife. 'He fired the shot and rode up here before he pumped another shell into the barrel of his gun. Prob'ly stopped his horse and looked back before he headed into the hills.'

The sheriff nodded solemnly.

'I'll tell you what I'm goin' to do; I'm goin' back to town and tell Van Avery to git to hell out of this country before somebody kills him.'

'I'm afraid he won't go,' replied Hashknife. 'That kid has been shot once and shot at twice; but he ain't scared yet.'

'He's crazy, I tell you.'

'No, he ain't crazy—he's nervy. You don't hear him squawkin' about that bullet along his ribs, and he ain't cryin' over bein' robbed. My opinion is that he's stuck on Elene Corey.'

'He ain't so dumb,' declared Sleepy. 'He's jist ignorant. Somebody ought to tell him that a bullet, properly placed, will kill him. Mebbe he thinks that people don't die from nothin' but old age.'

They went back to the house, and the sheriff talked with Mrs. Corey. There were cattle and horses to be taken care of, and the sheriff asked her what she intended doing.

'I don't know,' she admitted miserably. 'We can't afford to hire even one man. There is no market for cattle, and no one wants to buy a horse. What on earth are we going to do?'

'Shore tough,' admitted the sheriff. 'I don't even know what to advise you to do, Mrs. Corey.'

'We are up against a blank wall,' sighed the old

lady. 'I used to think I had lots of courage; but the last few days have taken it all away from me. I just go around in sort of a daze, wondering what will become of us all.'

Hashknife fingered his hat thoughtfully and finally looked at the old lady.

'You don't know anythin' about me and my pardner,' he said, 'but if you're willin' to take us for what we are, we'd like to help you out. Anyway, we could kinda tide you over. We both savvy horses and cows pretty well.'

'Well, that's shore generous,' said the sheriff quickly.

'You mean you would work for us, with no salary in sight?' asked the old lady wonderingly.

'If you could tolerate us—yes'm.'

'We're good cowhands,' added Sleepy. 'Only thing is, I've got a weakness for hotcakes like you had this mornin'.'

'Why, I don't know what to say,' said Mrs. Corey. 'I—I don't like to say no, and I hate to say yes. It isn't fair to you boys.'

'Plenty fair to us,' replied Hashknife quickly. 'All we ask you to do is quit worryin' so hard. Look at the doughnut instead of the hole inside it. No use worryin' about the things that might be, 'cause the things that we worry about the most hardly ever happen.'

'I reckon that's mighty good advice,' said the sheriff, getting to his feet and picking up his hat.

'And I'm shore glad these two boys are goin' to help you, Mrs. Corey. Mebbe that's the start of better luck.'

As he went down the steps into the patio, Handsome Hartwig, riding a lathered sorrel, came through the gate. It was evident that the little deputy had ridden fast. He slid off his horse and came toward the steps, panting a little.

'There's hell to pay at the Comanche Chief!' he blurted. 'Foreman murdered and thirty thousand dollars' worth of gold bars stolen. Steele jist got to town and reported; so I came to git you, Banty.'

'They killed Tommy Ryan?' asked the sheriff.

'Too dead to skin. Them bars was run yesterday afternoon. Steele said that Ryan slept in the office last night, guardin' the safe. But they got in on him and blew the safe. Nobody heard it.'

'What next?' growled the sheriff. 'This country's goin' to the dogs.'

Hashknife turned to Sleepy.

'You're punchin' cows for the Corey outfit alone until I git back from the Comanche Chief. I'm goin' to help the sheriff look at a busted safe and make bad guesses how it was done and who did it.'

'Hop on to it.' Sleepy grinned. 'I'll miss you, but it's all right.'

Back in Painted Wells, they found that Steele had taken the coroner back with him; so they hurried on the two miles to the Comanche Chief. Steele met them and took them into the office, where they found Doctor Smedley and the mine assayer, a little man wearing heavy glasses.

Work had been suspended and a crowd of curious miners loafed around outside the office. Several of them knew the sheriff and deputy. Tommy Ryan had been popular with the men, and they were anxious to find out more about the murder.

No one had touched Ryan's body, which was sprawled beside a cot, the blankets of which were in a heap on the floor. Ryan's huge body had been powerless against the two bullets, one in his chest, the other through his head.

The safe was a big old-fashioned affair. Its door sagged open. The sheriff and coroner busied themselves with the body, but, after a glance, Hashknife turned his attention to the safe.

Steele was saying: 'They got sixty ingots, damn their hides! Why, it was a hundred and twenty-five pounds of raw gold that they stole. But I'd have given it gladly if they had only let poor Tommy live. Here's his gun.'

Steele picked up a Colt .38 from the table and held it in his hand.

'They never gave him a chance in the world, the dirty devils!'

Hashknife came from the safe and looked at the gun. It was a double-action gun, police model.

Hashknife swung the cylinder out and looked at the cartridges. He snapped the gun shut, with a thoughtful expression in his eyes and handed it to the sheriff.

'You'll keep this for evidence, I reckon,' he said.

'Evidence?' queried the sheriff. 'Why, that was Ryan's gun.'

'I'd keep it,' said Hashknife, looking the sheriff square in the eye. 'You can't afford to overlook anythin' in a deal like this.'

'Shore,' muttered the sheriff, and he slipped the gun in his pocket.

It did not require much time for the sheriff and coroner to finish their examination. Steele had a number of the miners move the body to Ryan's quarters. A little later Hashknife and the sheriff rode back down toward Painted Wells.

'The hell of it is they didn't leave a danged clue,' complained the sheriff. 'It shore was a complete job, to my way of thinkin'.'

'What did you think of the blowin' of that safe?' asked Hashknife.

'Well they shore blowed it, Hartley. Poor Tommy, they never gave him a chance in the world. Too bad he didn't git a chance to do some shootin' himself.'

'I don't reckon he could—not even with the chance he had.'

'Chance he had?' grunted the sheriff. 'What do you mean?'

'Look at that gun you got in your pocket.'

Wondering what Hashknife meant, the sheriff looked at the gun.

'Open it,' said Hashknife.

The sheriff swung out the cylinder and studied the cartridges. He jerked up his head and looked wonderingly at Hashknife.

'My God!' he exclaimed. 'Two of these shells has been—why!'

He turned the cylinder, snapped it into place, and pulled the trigger. There was no report; just the dull click of the hammer.

'Even the primers are dummy,' said Hashknife. 'They never gave Ryan a ghost of a chance. Can you imagine how he felt when he snapped that gun twice and it wouldn't go off?'

'I never believed in capital punishment,' said the sheriff slowly, 'but I'd gladly stretch the rope for the man who done this.'

The following morning Silver Steele announced the closing of the Comanche Chief for an indefinite period, retaining only Jim Ortelle, the assayer, one shift boss, and two men to act as caretakers. Steele's only explanation was that under present conditions he was unable to operate at a profit.

The closing of the mine was a severe blow to Painted Wells, as Steele's payroll was quite heavy. Especially did it cut off a big revenue to Ed Ault, who was still in Phoenix.

'The worst of it is, we're in the richest stuff we ever had,' said Steele to the sheriff. 'But I'm not a millionaire; I can't stand losses of thirty thousand at a time. I haven't been makin' any money. Someday I'll operate again, but with an entirely new crew. Every man at the mine now is carryin' a Winchester, and they've got orders to use 'em. Ortelle is virtually in charge, and he picked out a hard crew for any higrader to buck against.'

CHAPTER V

Van Avery DISAPPEARS

Hashknife and Sleepy plunged into the work at the Diamond C. For two days they were busy repairing and greasing the three old wooden windmills, scattered far apart over the range, shifting a bunch of thirsty cattle from a dry water-hole to where they might get a long-delayed drink, butchering veal for consumption at the ranch.

They worked early and late—harder than they had ever worked for wages. Since the death of Milt Corey and the arrest of Ken Steele, there had been no one on the job at the Diamond C. On the third day Hashknife rode to town with Elene and her sister. He had never met Ken Steele, and Elene insisted on his going with them to the jail.

They had told Ken about Hashknife and Sleepy volunteering to help them at the ranch, so Ken gave Hashknife a hearty grip through the bars. Ken Steele was a capable-looking young man, well built and with a finely shaped head. He did not strike Hashknife as being the type of man who would commit murder.

'I dunno how we're ever goin' to thank you,' he

said to Hashknife, after he had greeted Elene and his wife affectionately.

'We ain't doin' much,' answered Hashknife, 'and Ma Corey's meals are plenty pay for us. Sleepy is gettin' hog-fat.'

'Don't try to belittle the work you have done,' said Elene. 'You've done more real work in two days than a dozen paid cowboys would have done. Are they treating you all right, Ken?'

'Oh, I suppose they're doin' the best they can. The prosecutin' attorney was in to visit me yesterday afternoon.'

'Did he have anything new to ask?' queried his wife anxiously.

Ken shook his head.

'Nothin' new, dear; he wanted me to confess. He said it would save the taxpayers a lot of money, and he'd see that I merely got life. He said I didn't have a chance in the world, anyway, so I might as well make it easy for everybody.'

'As I understand it,' said Hashknife, 'the only evidence against you is the fact that you knew Ault was to loan that money; that you started home ahead of Mr. Corey, and that your gun apparently was the weapon used.'

'That seems to be enough, doesn't it?' asked Ken bitterly. 'As a matter of fact, all I did was to act like a weak-kneed fool. I owed Ault a lot of money. My wife didn't know it, and I was ashamed to tell her. I came to town the night before, and Ault demanded money. I guess he knew Glad didn't know I owed it; so he threatened to tell her. He had already tried to get my father to pay the bill.

'Anyway, Ault and I had hard words. I didn't go home; I got drunk, and I think I made cracks about shootin' Ault. Mebbe I would have shot him, if the play came up right. Anyway, I kinda remember that somebody took my gun away from me. What there was left of the night, I guess I spent in the stable behind the Yucca Saloon, and it was noon before I woke up, sick as a fool.

'That one night sure cured me of drinkin'. I went down to the livery-stable and spent several hours on the stableman's cot. He got me a pot of strong coffee, and that put me on my feet. I went back to the Yucca Saloon, where I seen Dad Corey at the bar, talkin' with Ed Ault. Ault was countin' out some money. I didn't want Dad to see me; so I took my horse and headed for home.

'I was still sick and disgusted with myself. Just to show you how sick I was that day, I never missed my gun until I was almost home. I didn't remember right then about somebody takin' my gun away from me—that came later. I thought I lost it in the livery-stable; so I turned around and started back. But I didn't go far, because I was afraid I'd meet Dad Corey. I decided to go on home, and I did. No one saw me ride in; so they couldn't prove what time I did get there. I went into the bunkhouse and flopped down on a bunk.

'I must have went right to sleep, because that's where the sheriff found me; me there on the bunk, smelling of bad whiskey, and my holster empty. I should be here in jail for treatin' my wife the way I did; but God knows I never shot Dad Corey.'

Ken's story rang true to Hashknife. It was the first time he had heard any of Ken's side of the story.

'Do you remember who was with you when you said you'd kill Ault?' asked Hashknife.

'No, I don't, Hartley; that's the worst of it.'

'No idea who took your gun that night?'

'No. I remember tryin' to find it, and I remember arguin' with somebody about it.'

Hashknife turned to Handsome. 'Did you ever try to check up on who was with him that night?'

'Why would I?' asked Handsome. 'This is the first time I ever heard Ken tell about it. Doggone him, he ain't talked to anybody until now.'

'That's true,' said Ken. 'I was goin' to keep my mouth shut until I could tell it to a lawyer.'

Hashknife walked back into the sheriff's office, leaving the two girls with Ken and Handsome.

'Hello, Hathknife,' said a lisping voice.

Hashknife turned to see Van Avery seated against the wall, grinning. He looked funny with those missing teeth.

'Hello,' greeted Hashknife, 'how are you, Van?'

'Pretty good. Everybody all right at the ranth?

I wanted to thee you, and I thaw you coming in a while ago and—thay, did you ever lothe two teeth. I thound like hell, don't I?'

Hashknife laughed as they walked outside.

'Never mind the teeth.'

Van Avery led him away from the office and grew confidential. He had found out that the credit of the Diamond C was badly strained at the general store, and that the bank had started foreclosure proceedings on the Diamond C. It seemed that Van Avery had wired for more funds, had received them by telegraph, and had opened an account at the bank.

'You ain't aimin' to stay here, are you?' asked Hashknife.

Van Avery most certainly was. He had been out to the Comanche Chief mine with Silver Steele, inspecting the workings and examining the safe.

'Mithter Thteele wath awful kind to me,' he said. 'I thaw everything there wath to thee, and I had thupper at the ranth.'

Hashknife looked at him gravely.

'Listen to me, kid,' he said seriously. 'You're cuttin' a tombstone for yourself and you don't realize it. Silver Steele thinks you are a detective in disguise, sent here to find out who is responsible for stealin' his valuable gold ore. He had one in here awhile back, and he was murdered. They smashed in his head and threw him into a hole. That's why somebody has been tryin' to kill you. Now, have a little sense and get out of here before it's too late.'

Van Avery looked blankly at Hashknife.

'That thertainly ith funny,' he said.

'It may be funny to you, but it ain't a damn bit funny to me,' said Hashknife. 'You're a nice kid and you mean well; but this gang of murderin' thieves will git you shore, like they got Payzant and Ryan.'

'I wath at the inquetht,' said Van Avery simply.

'Yeah, and the first thing you know you'll be the main character in another one.'

'I bought another gun,' said Van Avery. 'I've lotht two already.'

Hashknife shook his head sadly and held out his hand to Van Avery.

'Good luck,' he said seriously. 'If you won't use brains, you'll have to depend on luck.'

Hashknife left him in front of the store and went back to meet the two girls at the buckboard. Van Avery had gone into the store.

'Wasn't that Mr. Van Avery?' asked Elene.

'The Arizona target,' amended Hashknife as they got into the buckboard.

'You don't like him?' asked Elene.

'I never said that, Miss Corey.'

'I wish he'd come out to the ranch,' said Gladys. 'He is the most amusing person I ever saw.'

'Dumb,' declared Hashknife.

'I think he is a nice boy,' stated Elene. 'He may have queer ideas of things, but it is because he doesn't understand. He doesn't claim to be brilliant.'

Back at the ranch Hashknife told Ken's story to Sleepy, who was repairing a broken place in the corral fence.

'Sounds reasonable,' admitted Sleepy. 'I had a long talk with Ma Corey, and I tell you they're up against it hard. Would you believe it, they ain't got *no* money at all. Unless somethin' breaks, they'll be on a straight diet of beef.'

Sleepy threw the hatchet outside the corral and hitched up his belt.

'This is the first time I ever cursed the lack of money,' he said. 'She's as nice a old lady as I ever knowed. Don't squawk. She says that the Lord will provide. I said, "Yeah, that's all right, but—" What's this comin' our way, Hashknife?'

It was apparently a heavy wagon drawn by four horses, with two men on the seat. Hashknife shaded his eyes and watched them come in at the big gate.

'Big an' li'l fishes!' muttered Sleepy. 'That's Cornelius!'

Hashknife got a good look at the load of provisions and turned to Sleepy.

'The Lord has provided,' he said dryly. 'He worked through an agent, but here it is.'

They walked back to the corral and watched

the driver start to unload. Van Avery entered the house; in a few minutes he came out with the three women. After a brief conversation he walked down to the corral. There was a queer expression in his eyes, and he did not speak to the two cowboys. Sleepy was whittling on the top pole of the corral, paying no attention to the young man who leaned against the corral fence.

'You'd think I did thomething,' Van Avery finally muttered.

Hashknife reached over and put a hand on his shoulder.

'Van, I take back everythin' I ever said or thought about you.'

'I—I juth wanted to replath the thalt I thpilled—and it grew to a wagonload,' he said slowly. 'Darn it, I with I had a couple of good teeth. I thound like a four-year-old.'

'You sound like a hell of a big man to me,' said Hashknife seriously. 'And I'm bettin' Ma Corey thinks the same.'

Van Avery nodded, a little shamefaced.

'I gueth tho. I wonder if it would be thafe for me to stay to thupper?'

'Damn right!' blurted Sleepy. 'We'll set outside and shoot every damn person that comes close. You ain't got nothin' else to do; so why don'tcha stay out here and help us run the ranch?'

'I gueth I better not; you'd be thafer with me in town.'

Elene approached, and the conversation stopped. Hashknife looked meaningly at Sleepy, and the two cowboys drifted quickly around to the stable, leaving Elene and Van Avery together.

Ten minutes later, Van Avery joined Hashknife and Sleepy. Elene went back to the house.

'How are you?' asked Sleepy, for want of something better to say.

'I'm thad,' replied Van Avery.

'What makes you sad, pardner?'

'You'd be thad too, if you tried to be therious with two teeth out.'

Van Avery wouldn't stay for supper. He insisted that he must go back to Painted Wells; so Sleepy took him back in the buckboard. He did not go back to the house before leaving, and Hashknife wondered what had happened. He found Elene alone in the patio and told her that Van Avery had gone back to town.

Elene turned away for several moments; when she looked at Hashknife again her eyes were filled with tears.

'It was all my fault.' She choked, halfway between laughing and crying. 'He—he was serious, and I laughed. Oh, I shall never forgive myself for doing that.'

She wiped away her tears and started for the porch.

'Mind tellin' me about it?' asked Hashknife. 'Mebbe we can fix it up some way.'

'I'm afraid not,' she replied. 'You see, he pro-posed to me—kinda. He—he said, "I'm going to marry you if thomebody don't thoot me too thoon." '

Hashknife laughed, then turned toward the gate.

'No, I don't reckon I'd be any help,' he said. 'Don't you worry. If he don't come back, he ain't worth your answer.'

'But I don't want to marry anybody,' Elene said.

'That's fine; I'll tell him.'

'You don't need to bother yourself,' she said curtly as she went into the house.

Hashknife chuckled softly to himself on his way down to the stable to feed the horses.

The next morning Elene asked Hashknife to take her to town. She was perfectly frank about it.

'I want to apologize to Mr. Van Avery,' she said. 'Neither mother nor Glad know why he went away yesterday without saying a word to them; I want him to know I'm sorry for laughing.'

But they did not find Avery in Painted Wells. The proprietor of the hotel said that Van Avery did not sleep there during the night. His stuff was still in the room, the rent of which was paid for a week. Neither the sheriff nor the deputy was able to tell where he had gone.

'I seen him about seven o'clock,' said Handsome. 'He was settin' on the sidewalk in front of the hotel.'

Silver Steele was in town, so Hashknife questioned him, thinking that Van Avery might have gone out to the JS Ranch. But Steele had not seen him for two days.

Hashknife was frankly worried about Van Avery. He talked with the sheriff, who was of the opinion that the men who had tried to shoot Van Avery had lured him out of town with the intention of putting him out of the way.

Investigation proved that he did not go away on the stage, and a search of his room disclosed the fact that he did not wear his big hat, boots, or chaps. On the table were his cartridge belt and empty holster.

'I'll see what I can do toward findin' him,' said the sheriff, as they went back to the street. 'But I'm scared they've got him this time.'

Elene visited Ken for a few minutes, then they went back to the ranch. Sleepy wanted to search for Van Avery, but he admitted that he didn't know just where to look.

About mid-afternoon the sheriff rode out to the ranch. He was going to Red Hill and wondered whether Hashknife didn't want to ride down with him. Hashknife assented.

Mrs. Corey told the sheriff about Van Avery's bringing a load of provisions out to them.

'I know he did, Mrs. Corey; and that's one

reason I'm goin' to try and find him. There ain't many fellers like that in the world, and we can't afford to lose what we've got. He ain't very bright, but he's shore good-hearted. We might pick up some trace of him in Red Hill, and that's why I want Hartley to go along. You know'—confidentially—'there's a feller that ain't dumb.'

'I think Mr. Hartley is one of God's gentlemen,' said Mrs. Corey.

'Well, I dunno about that. But he's plenty smart.'

The long, dusty ride was without incident. They did not hurry, and it was supper-time when they reached Red Hill. At a little restaurant they met Steve McCord, owner of the X8X outfit at Porcupine, and Brad Thatcher, one of McCord's cowboys. McCord was a big, hard-faced cattle-man, slightly gray, with cold blue eyes and a square chin. Brad Thatcher was below medium height, wiry, thin-faced, possibly thirty years of age. One eye was slightly off line, which gave him a squinting expression.

The sheriff knew them both very well. It developed that McCord was the one who had sent the telegram about Van Avery's holding-up the poker game. Hashknife noticed that McCord did not appreciate the sheriff's explanation as to why he did not catch the holdup man.

'That's all right, Banty,' said McCord. 'We happen to know you didn't try very hard.'

The big sheriff laughed at McCord.

'You ort to be glad I didn't, Steve. Imagine you and your gang on the witness stand, testifyin' that this tenderfoot held you up and took his money back, because you tried to higrade him out of a pot.'

Steve's retort was unprintable. He hammered on the table and swore no one stole that card.

'Yeah, and then one of you tried to shoot this kid through a car winder,' accused the sheriff.

'He told you that, did he?'

'He didn't need to,' said Hashknife. 'I was on that car.'

'Yeah?' McCord sized Hashknife up closely. 'You was, eh?'

'Nothin' wrong about that, is there?'

'What's use arguin' about ancient hist'ry?' interrupted Thatcher.

'And if it's any news to you,' said the sheriff, 'that kid has disappeared.'

'He has, eh?' grunted McCord, a glint of amusement in his eyes. 'If it's any news to me, eh? I don't like that remark, Brayton. You speak as though I had somethin' to do with him disappearin'.'

Banty Brayton's jaw jutted a trifle as he leaned across the table, shoving the dishes aside.

'Lemme tell you somethin', Steve. One of your men shot at this kid through a car winder. The next day the stage was held up, and somebody shot this kid down. They thought they had killed him, and they took two thousand dollars off him. A few nights ago some dirty murderer shot through the dinin'-room winder of the Diamond C ranch-house with a .45-70 rifle, tryin' to kill the kid.

'I'm not accusin' anybody, you understand; but the trouble started in Porcupine. Nobody in Red Hill or Painted Wells ever had any trouble with the kid. There shore wasn't any reason for shootin' him down at the holdup, 'cause the kid didn't have any gun and he never made any move as though he had a gun. That shot through the ranch-house winder was a deliberate attempt to murder him.'

'You ain't tryin' to put the deadwood on me, are you?' asked Steve coldly. 'As a matter of fact, you don't know that me or one of my men shot through that car window. You're jist guessin', Banty.'

'Did he have trouble with anybody else in Porcupine?'

'I don't know a damn thing about him. But I'll tell you this much, Brayton; don't start accusin' me and my gang, until you get a lot more evidence than you've got now.'

'Like I said at first, I'm not accusin' you nor anybody else,' said the sheriff calmly. 'I jist merely wanted you to know that the kid is missin'; and if you should happen to run across him, you might see that he gits back to Painted Wells all right.'

'Is Painted Wells so damn hard up for men that you crave this soft-boiled aig?' asked Thatcher sarcastically.

'Keep out of it, Brad,' advised McCord.

'You fellers play a pretty stiff game at Porcupine, don'tcha?' asked Hashknife. 'These here thousand-dollar pots look kinda heavy for a cowtown game.'

'You might come over and turn a few cards sometime,' suggested McCord. 'We allus aim to please our visitors.'

'Yeah, I might,' said Hashknife seriously. 'I dunno jist what I'd use for money, but I might come, anyway. I like to see a big game, even if I ain't got money enough to buy a stack of whites.'

The sheriff laughed, as he attacked his meal.

'Don't let 'em git you down, Hashknife,' he said. 'They play a four-bits-a-stack game, table stakes, and howl like a coyote if you quit two dollars winner. I know 'em well.'

'You ain't feelin' good tonight, are you, Banty?' asked McCord. 'You might at least say somethin' good about Porcupine.'

'Porcupine's all right; all they need is a better class of people.'

'That's all hell needs,' grunted Hashknife.

McCord paid for his and Thatcher's meal and stopped in the doorway as he left.

'Come over and see us sometime,' he said. 'We'll show you a good time.'

'Thank you,' replied the sheriff, his mouth full of food. 'I've been over there.'

'Anyway, we almost made 'em mad,' chuckled the sheriff after the two men had gone.

'Was that your idea?' asked Hashknife.

'I dunno. McCord allus rubs me the wrong way, and I thought I had a chance to hand some of it back to him. If I had a hunch that the kid was over at Porcupine, I'd go over there in a minute.'

Hashknife nodded thoughtfully.

'So would I. Brayton, do you think for a minute that McCord and his gang are mixed up in these attempts to kill Van Avery?'

'Why would they be? All he done was take back some money they tried to steal from him. McCord don't strike me as a feller that would pull off a sneakin' murder jist because a feller defended his own. How does he strike you, Hashknife?'

'Plenty forked.'

After their supper, Hashknife left the sheriff at the saloon, talking with the bartender, and went up to the depot. The agent did not remember selling a ticket to anyone of Van Avery's description. He hadn't sold any tickets to strangers during the past month.

'Do you know Ed Ault?' asked Hashknife.

'Sure, I know him. He bought a ticket to Phoenix a few days ago.'

Hashknife went back to the saloon and joined the sheriff. Their trip had netted them nothing, except to convince them that Van Avery, alive or dead, was still in the county.

As they rode back toward Painted Wells, Hashknife asked the sheriff if Handsome had told him what Ken Steele had explained about someone taking his gun away the night before the murder.

'Yeah, I heard about that,' said the sheriff.

'Didja try to find out who was drinkin' with Ken that night?'

'I ain't tried yet.'

'Try it. Find the man who took that gun, and we'll have a darned good chance to put the deadwood on somebody.'

'Are you turnin' detective?' queried the sheriff.

'Don't forget that Silver Steele will give five thousand dollars for proof that Ken didn't kill Corey.'

'I'm afraid nobody will ever collect that money, Hashknife. That gun will convict Ken as sure as the devil. No jury will believe his story.'

'Prob'ly not. How far from the body did you find the gun?'

'Oh, mebbe fifteen, twenty feet, layin' in some weeds.'

'Are you sure it is Ken's gun?'

'Absolutely. Why, it's got his initials on it.'

Hashknife laughed softly.

'What's funny about it?' demanded the sheriff.

'Why did he throw his gun away?'

'Why, I dunno. It was all over blood.'

'Could have been washed, couldn't it?'

'Shore, but—'

'Brayton, use what little sense God gave you. Would any halfway intelligent person commit murder with a marked gun and throw the gun away near the body?'

'He admits he was drunk.'

'He admits he was sick. That gun was planted there to throw suspicion on Ken. Brayton, the murderer was in Painted Wells, and he saw Ken leave town ahead of Milt Corey. Who he was, I don't know. He had the gun which was taken away from Ken. Very likely he would have killed Milt Corey anyway, but this was a dandy chance to shift suspicion to Ken. He murdered Corey, threw the gun aside where you'd find it, and pulled out with the ten thousand dollars.'

Brayton rode along silently for quite a while.

'I reckon the drinks are on Silver Steele,' he said.

'What do you mean?'

'Thinkin' that young Van Avery was the detective.'

'All right, Brayton; but we'll keep on thinkin' Van Avery is the detective until we know better.'

'Suits me jist right, Hashknife.'

• • •

When Silver Steele retained Judge William Frazer to defend his son, he secured the services of a criminal lawyer who would fight to the last ditch. It would be two weeks until the next term of court, which was little enough time to prepare a defense. The judge arrived in Painted Wells two days after Hashknife and the sheriff had been to Red Hill. He knew nothing about the case, but it did not require much time for him to get an idea of things. He had a talk with Ken, and afterward talked with Ed Ault, who had come back from his trip a day ahead of the judge's arrival.

The judge intimated that he wanted to talk with Mrs. Corey. Ault offered to take him out to the ranch, which arrangement was acceptable to the judge. Elene had decided to ride with Hashknife and Sleepy that day, and they were away from the ranch. Gladys saw Ault with the stranger, and refused to come downstairs; so Ault twiddled his thumbs alone on the porch while the judge talked with Mrs. Corey in the ranch-house.

It was after the interview, while Mrs. Corey was talking with the judge and Ault on the porch, that Ault mentioned the fact that it was kind of Hartley and Stevens to help them out.

'I don't know what I would have done without them,' said the old lady. 'They are just doing everything for us. Even in Arizona, I didn't know

109

there are men like those two. Hashknife Hartley is—'

'Pardon me,' interrupted the judge. 'Did you say Hashknife Hartley, Mrs. Corey?'

'Yes.'

'Well, well!' exclaimed the judge softly. 'Hashknife Hartley!'

'Do you know him?' asked Ault curiously.

'Not personally. Hmmm!'

'Anything wrong about him?' asked Ault.

'Wrong?' The judge chuckled. 'Not that I have ever heard, Mr. Ault. In fact, it is just the reverse. Mrs. Corey, I wish you would have him get in touch with me. Perhaps he has never heard of me. Our paths have never crossed, but we have mutual friends.'

'I shall be glad to tell him,' said Mrs. Corey.

'Thank you kindly, madam; it is a favor to me.'

Ault was curious. Why would this lawyer want to see Hashknife Hartley? He waited until they were nearly back to Painted Wells before he asked any questions, and he led up to them with—

'Hartley is quite a character, Judge.'

'Character? Oh, yes, I suppose he is. Rather wonderful character.'

'I didn't think he was an ordinary cow-puncher.'

'No, I'd say he was rather extraordinary. How long has he been here?'

110

'Oh, not very long. Says he's lookin' over range land for some packin'-house in the East.'

'Ummm, yes, I suppose he is. Wasn't here at the time of Corey's death, was he?'

'No. He came here at the same time Elene Corey came home. Same train, I reckon.'

The judge was silent for a while. Suddenly he snapped the question—

'Did you know Payzant?'

'Not by that name,' replied Ault. 'We knew him as Jack Cherry.'

'I see. Queer situation here. Sheriff told me about this Van Avery, supposedly a detective. Devil of a mess.'

'Think you can build up a defense for Ken Steele?' asked Ault.

'Mr. Ault, the best defense in the world is to prove that somebody else committed the crime.'

'I'm afraid you've got a job on your hands, Judge.' Ault laughed.

'Job? Oh, certainly. Expected a job. Feel better about it now.'

'With Hashknife Hartley in the country, eh?' queried Ault.

'You folks need rain out here. Country is awful dry.'

Mrs. Corey told Hashknife about the judge and Ed Ault's being out there, and that the judge wanted to see him. She told of the conversation on the porch, and of the judge's surprise at knowing who was working on the ranch.

Elene was watching the expression on Hashknife's face; after her mother had gone in the house she went to him.

'What is wrong?' she asked softly.

Hashknife looked at her and shook his head.

'Everythin' is all right, Elene,' he said.

'You don't know this Judge Frazer?'

'I never heard of him. Shucks, there's lots of folks I never heard about.'

'Can his knowing you hurt you in any way?'

'I hope not.'

'Won't you tell me what it means, Hashknife? You know we'd do anything in the world for you and Sleepy.'

'Well, bless your heart'—Hashknife smiled— 'it's all right. We ain't done anythin' wrong. This is jist one time when we should have changed our names, tha's all.'

'You didn't want the judge to know who you are?'

Hashknife was silent for several minutes. Finally he asked—

'Elene, would you trust Ed Ault?'

'I would not.'

'He heard what was said, and he prob'ly heard more from the lawyer. But don't worry about us. I better go and wash my face.'

'Oh, I'm so sorry Mother mentioned your name.'

'Keep smilin'. Everythin' is goin' great. As Sleepy would say, "I'm afraid everythin' is goin' to be all right."'

Hashknife found Sleepy down at the corral and told him what had been said. Sleepy screwed up his face seriously and whistled through his teeth.

'Makes it kinda tough,' he said. 'From now on we better look jist a little out. It all depends on how open-mouthed that lawyer got about us on the way back to town. I don't like Ault. He's smooth, like a snake. Mebbe he's all right, though.'

'Mebbe. Somebody around here is all wrong, and it might not be Ault. But you can't keep a man from talkin'.'

'You shore can't. Are you goin' in to see the Judge?'

'Be a good thing, I suppose. If the beans ain't all spilled, we might save a few.'

'Oh, well.' Sleepy took off his hat and mopped his brow with his sleeve. 'I'm jist scared to death that everythin' is goin' to be all right.'

CHAPTER VI
HASHKNIFE PROSPECTS

Hashknife said no more about going in to see the lawyer until after dark that night, when he and Sleepy went down to the stable, saddled their horses and rode into the hills. They were both afraid that the traveled roads were dangerous for them now, and they were taking no chances.

They tied their horses to a fence behind the hotel and went around to the door. It was a few minutes past nine o'clock, but the street was deserted. They went into the hotel and found the proprietor tilted back in a chair behind his little counter, reading a paper-back novel.

'Well, glad to see you back, boys.' He smiled genially. 'How's everythin'?'

'Goin' along fine,' said Hashknife. 'I reckon Judge Frazer is stoppin' here, ain't he?'

'Oh, yeah; he's in No. 10. Pretty nice sort of a feller, he is.'

'Is he in his room now?'

'Must be. Come in after supper and said he had a lot of writin' to do; so I give him a extra lamp. Didja want to see him?'

'He wanted to see us,' replied Hashknife.

'Well, I reckon it's all right. Want me to take you up?'

'We can find No. 10.'

'Shore—go ahead.'

The narrow hallway was dark, but there was light shining from under the door of No. 10. Hashknife knocked softly. There was no reply and no sound from anyone in the room. Another knock failed to elicit a reply.

'Must have gone out and left his lamp burnin',' said Sleepy.

Hashknife turned the knob. The door opened. Both lamps were burning, and sprawled on the floor, his head and shoulders under the bed, was Judge Frazer. There was blood on the bed, a splatter of it across the little table and on some sheets of writing-paper.

Hashknife quickly turned the man over. His head and shoulders were a mass of gore, and it looked as though his head had been battered to a pulp, but he was still alive.

'Get the sheriff and have him find the doctor as quick as you can, Sleepy,' ordered Hashknife.

Sleepy ran down the stairs, much to the amazement of the old man at the desk; and within ten minutes the sheriff, deputy, and Doctor Smedley were there, together with the proprietor. No one else knew what had happened.

'Be a job to save him,' declared the doctor. 'Get some clean bedding; we'll keep him here. No use moving him. Get me a lot of hot water.'

'Think you can save him?' asked Hashknife.

'Make a try at it,' panted the doctor. 'Damn bad beating they gave him. Looks as though they tried to hammer his head off. What's this country coming to, anyway? Where's that hot water?'

The sheriff, grim of face, drew Hashknife out into the hallway. He knew that Judge Frazer had been retained to defend Ken, but he did not know anything further. They walked to the end of the hallway, where some stairs led down to the rear of the building near the kitchen entrance.

Hashknife told of the judge's visit at the ranch with Ault, adding that the judge had left word that he wanted Hashknife to come to see him.

'We came to see what he wanted, and you see what we found,' said Hashknife.

'Why did he want to see you, Hashknife?'

'He didn't say. He told Mrs. Corey that me and him had mutual friends, and he wanted to see me.'

There was moonlight, and from where they stood it was easy to see their two horses tied to the old fence.

'Your broncs?' asked the sheriff.

'Yeah.'

'How'd you come to tie 'em out there?'

'We came in through the hills and didn't bother to ride around to the street.'

'Through the hills? You mean you didn't come on the road?'

'The road don't come through the hills, does it?'

The sheriff was silent for several moments. Then—

'I'm gettin' scared too.'

They walked back, and the sheriff questioned the hotel-keeper. No one had gone through the office since the judge came in. He was sure of that. No, he had not heard any noises. Leaving Handsome to assist the doctor, Hashknife, Sleepy, and the sheriff went over to the Yucca Saloon. The usual crowd was there. Ed Ault was running a roulette wheel. He nodded to the three of them.

'Not much of a crowd tonight,' said Hashknife to the bartender as he poured their drinks.

'Jist average,' replied the drink-dispenser. 'The closing-down of the Comanche Chief sure slowed up business for this place. I wonder if there's any chance of Steele's startin' it up again.'

'Not for a while,' replied the sheriff. 'I notice that Steele's lawyer is here gettin' ready to defend Ken.'

'Yes, he was here this afternoon. Looks plenty smart, and they say he's great on murder cases.'

'That's his reputation.' The sheriff nodded.

'Been any of the boys over from Porcupine?' asked Hashknife.

'McCord and Ike Berry was here. Come over to get some stuff from Nelson, I guess. They left about four o'clock.'

'That was after Ault and the lawyer got back from the Diamond C, wasn't it?'

'I'm not sure. Yeah, I think it was. You might ask Ault.'

They finished their drinks and left the place, going back to the hotel where the doctor had patched up the lawyer as well as he could.

'Here's his card and address, Banty,' said the doctor. 'You better wire his family.'

'Pretty bad, eh?'

'He's about as bad as they ever get, and still be alive. I'll stay with him tonight.'

Hashknife and Sleepy slipped back to their horses and rode home in the moonlight, but not on the road.

'Why did they try to kill him?' asked Sleepy. 'He wasn't no detective; he was jist a lawyer. Hashknife, I don't savvy it at all.'

'Gallows bait, Sleepy. They'll kill anybody who might put the deadwood on them. They can't quit now. The only life that means anythin' now is their own. Whoever they are, they killed Milt Corey. I don't know what Frazer knew, but he must have known somethin'—and he was foolish enough to talk.'

'Yeah, and if we get out of this with a whole skin, I'll shore give three cheers,' said Sleepy. 'I wonder what they done to poor Blondy Van Avery.'

They inspected the ranch buildings cautiously before stabling their horses. The Corey family were still waiting up for them, and they listened with amazement to the story of what had happened to the old lawyer.

None of them could understand why the lawyer should have been the object of a murderous attack; but as Sleepy and Hashknife were starting out to the bunkhouse, Elene said to Hashknife—

'Could it have been because he knew you?'

Hashknife shook his head thoughtfully.

'I'd hate to think that, Elene. You see, I don't know who Frazer talked with or what he might have said. Unless he lives and saves his memory, we prob'ly never will know. Jist knowin' me hadn't ought to be cause for anybody tryin' to kill him.'

'Oh, I didn't mean it that way, Hashknife.'

'I know what you meant,' he said, patting her on the shoulder. 'Don't worry.'

'You'll be careful, won't you?'

'Me? I'm the most careful person you ever met. If I hadn't been, I'd have been killed off a long time ago.'

'There is nothing yet about Van Avery?'

Hashknife shook his head sadly.

'Not a thing. You liked that kid.'

'We all liked him, Hashknife. He was different, but—'

'I know; I like 'em different myself. Good night.'

Early the following morning the sheriff rode out to the ranch. Frazer was still alive. The sheriff

119

said he was up half the night answering telegrams and arguing with the stage station agent, who was also the telegraph operator.

'They're sendin' a expert surgeon from Phoenix,' said the sheriff. 'All I hope is that there's somethin' to work on after he gits here. After you left last night, I got to pokin' around in his room. It looked to me as though he had been writin' a letter when they interrupted him.

'Anyway, the bottle of ink was spilled all over some papers, and the papers was on the floor. Here's one that looks like part of a letter, but most of it was so soaked with ink you couldn't read it.'

He handed Hashknife part of a page of notepaper, the edges gummed with ink. The top and bottom of the letter were missing, having been soaked to pulp by the ink and pulled off; so there was no chance to discover to whom it was written. It read:

—the name of that expert safecracker you sent up for five years, about six years ago? I'm not so clear on the sentence. Unless I am mistaken, Evans and Crowninshield defended him. Perhaps you will remember him, because he nearly made his escape after his conviction. Seems to me his name was Fillmore. I'm asking, because there . . .

And there the letter ended. Hashknife rubbed his chin and looked at the sheriff.

'Almost,' he said sadly. 'Damn that ink!'

'Almost what?' asked the sheriff blankly.

'Almost a chance to put our finger on the man who blew that safe at the Comanche Chief. Banty, that job was done by an expert.'

'Yeah? What makes you think it was?'

'No inexperienced man could do it. The man who blew that safe knew to a drop how much nitroglycerin it took to open the door. He knew where to put it and how to shoot it off.'

'I imagine you're right, Hashknife. Who do you reckon loaded that gun for Ryan?'

'Who knows?'

'Well, damn it, I want to know!' snorted the sheriff. 'I tell you, this is gettin' on my nerves. Who killed Payzant? Who killed Ryan? Who got away with Van Avery? Who tried to murder Frazer? I asked Handsome this mornin' what in hell we're goin' to do, and he said we might set down and keep tally. Damn fool makes me mad.'

Hashknife frowned.

'I wish I could help you, Banty; but I'm jist a cowpuncher.'

Hashknife felt sorry for the sheriff, Banty Brayton was as honest as a dollar, and very conscientious; but his mind ran in a single track. Perhaps at this time it ran on no track at all.

'Didja find out who was with Ken Steele the

night before the murder?' asked Hashknife.

'No, I didn't,' admitted the sheriff. 'I been a-layin' off to do that.'

'You ought to wait awhile longer and mebbe they'll tell it to their grandchildren.'

'I know—' sadly. 'Hell, I'm all muddled. Can't remember what to do next, I'll let you know what I find out.'

'I'm not your superior officer. Why tell me? Go ahead and work it out for yourself.'

'Why, I thought you wanted to know.'

'Go ahead. You find out, tell me who it was, and mebbe we'll work out somethin'. The right answer might git you elected again, Banty.'

'Nothin' will ever git me elected agin, Hashknife. I ain't goin' to quit as long as there's any leather left to pull; but I'm goin' to be damn sure what I climb onto next time.'

After the sheriff had gone back to town, Hashknife sat down and tried to puzzle out a few things. There was no doubt in his mind that the lawyer had recognized someone in Painted Wells who greatly resembled an ex-safecracker. In fact, it must have been more than a resemblance if the suspect sneaked into the lawyer's room and attempted to murder him. The question was— who might that man be?

Hashknife was satisfied that Van Avery had been mistaken for a detective, and it was very evident that this bad bunch would not hesitate to murder any detective suspect. Ryan's murder was no mystery. He had made an attempt to protect those golden ingots. Of course, his gun had been rendered useless by someone closely connected with the company, working with the bad bunch.

But Hashknife's reflections always drifted back to Payzant, the first victim of the gang. No doubt Payzant was familiar with his job. He impersonated a lone prospector and even went to the trouble of locating property. Hashknife could find no evidence that Payzant had ever been around the Comanche Chief; and it seemed to Hashknife that Payzant knew the main evidence was not to be found there.

He wondered if Payzant had been killed at Rick Nelson's prospect hole; or had he been carried there and thrown into the hole, after being struck over the head? Was there any significance to his being left there? Hashknife knew little about mines or minerals, but an irresistible hunch seemed to urge him to investigate that spot thoroughly.

He saddled his horse, told Sleepy to stay at the ranch, then rode over to the north line fence. He found Milt Corey's location notices, looked over his assessment work and examined the character of the rock. The rock meant nothing to Hashknife, so his examination was brief. He did examine the location notice, and observed that the claims ran only as far north as the fence line. Apparently

Corey's idea was merely to prevent Nelson from locating on the Diamond C property.

There was no location notice near the hole where Payzant's body had been found; but after considerable search Hashknife found it farther to the north. Checking up the approximate length of the claim, Hashknife decided that it ran to Corey's line fence. That is, Nelson's and Corey's claims joined at the fence.

At Nelson's location, which was marked as 'point of discovery,' Nelson had hardly scratched the ground. Hashknife went back to the prospect hole, where he sat down and smoked a cigarette. The hole was too deep for him to get down without the aid of a ladder or a rope. As far as he could see, there was no use going down there. The rock was all a dark brown, semidecomposed stuff.

Hashknife picked up a small piece and broke it against another piece of rock. He knew nothing about gold-bearing ores, but he put a small piece of the broken rock in his pocket and went back to the ranch, where he was rather surprised to find Silver Steele on the shady porch with Mrs. Corey.

Mrs. Corey called to Hashknife, who joined them, shaking hands with Steele.

'It has been years and years since Mr. Steele was here,' said the little old lady.

'A long, long time,' admitted Steele. 'Poor Milt hated me. From his viewpoint, I guess he had a right to hate me. I'll admit I took advantage of him, but at that time it looked like business. Rick Nelson swears he made an accurate assay of the samples Milt gave him. Anyway, after Milt gave up the prospect, Rick came to me and asked me how much I would give him for some sure-fire information on a quartz mine. He said it was free milling stuff, but he didn't have the money to develop it.

'He wanted ten thousand dollars, but I laughed at him. We finally made a deal, in which I was to give him half of the first twenty-thousand I grossed from the mine. That money was paid long ago. I accused Rick of making false reports to Milt, but he swore the reports were accurate and that he merely guessed there was gold in the Comanche Chief. I suppose he has kicked himself many a time for letting me have it for the ten thousand.'

'That is all past,' said Mrs. Corey.

'I'm glad you feel that way about it,' replied Steele. 'Milt would never listen to me.'

'They tell me you threw your kid out because he married Gladys Corey,' reminded Hashknife.

Steele's leathery face flushed.

'I did,' he said at length. 'Milt Corey was still alive, and I suppose I hated him for what he had said about me. I admit I didn't want Ken to marry Gladys. Not that Gladys wasn't too darn good for him, but because she was a Corey. I acted like a fool. Yes, I did, and I'll admit it now.'

'Confession is good for the soul,' murmured Mrs. Corey.

'I hope it helps mine.' He turned to Hashknife. 'What do you think about the attack on Judge Frazer last night?'

Hashknife shrugged his shoulders.

'What do you think?' he countered.

'I talked with the sheriff,' replied Steele. 'He's all muddled, and I'll admit I am. He spoke about Ryan's gun bein' loaded with blank cartridges; showed me the gun. He said you discovered it, and I remember you askin' him to keep the gun for evidence. He said you asked him to try and find out who was with Ken the night before Milt Corey was killed. Hartley, are you a detective?'

Hashknife smiled slowly.

'Mebbe the sheriff took me too seriously, Steele. Anyone could discover the things I've pointed out to him. Two of the cartridges in Ryan's gun had been struck by the hammer. That was a simple thing to discover. Ken told his story of what happened the night before Milt Corey was killed; he said he was drunk, talked about killin' Ault, and remembers that somebody took his gun away. I told the sheriff to find out who got that gun; at least, to find out who was with Ken and, if possible, to find out who left Painted Wells ahead of both Ken and Milt Corey.'

'You mean they stole Ken's gun to throw the blame on him?'

'The man who eventually got Ken's gun was the man who killed Milt Corey. As I see it, he knew Ault was to loan that money. Ken says he saw Milt Corey in the saloon gettin' the money. He didn't want Corey to see him in town; so he got on his horse and headed for home. The man who had Ken's gun saw Ken ride past; so he used Ken's gun and left it for evidence.'

'Good Lord!' exclaimed Steele. 'If you can prove who that man was, I'll give you five thousand dollars!'

Hashknife smiled grimly.

'Detectives don't last long around here.'

'It begins to look that way, Hartley. Where in the world is Van Avery?'

'I reckon we'd all like to know that.'

'Do you think he's a detective?' asked Steele.

'No, I don't reckon he is. Somebody thinks he is, though, that's a cinch.'

'He was out to see me, and I showed him over the mine. He examined the safe and talked about Ryan, but he was more interested in Payzant.'

'Interested in Payzant?'

'Quite a bit, it seems. He asked me all about how we found him and how long he had been dead, and if I felt sure he had been murdered.'

'I don't believe he ever mentioned Payzant to me,' said Hashknife.

'You didn't know anythin' about him, did you?'

'No, that's true. I didn't.'

'Do you think Judge Frazer will live?' asked Mrs. Corey.

'Well, he's still alive, Mrs. Corey. They're rushin' a surgeon from Phoenix, I hear. I hired Frazer because he is a dandy criminal lawyer. I wanted the best for Ken. Now I'm stumped. Court convenes next week and there's a short docket, which means that Ken's case will start soon; and I haven't a lawyer for him.'

Hashknife dug down in his pocket and drew out a piece of brown ore, which he handed to Steele.

'Does that look like anything to you?' he asked.

Silver Steele looked the piece over carefully, broke it with his fingers and looked closely at it. His eyes shifted to Hashknife.

'Where did you get that?' he asked.

'Picked it up,' replied Hashknife, evading an answer.

'Up at the Comanche Chief?'

'Is it that good?' queried Hashknife indifferently.

Steele laughed shortly and handed it back to Hashknife.

'Comes pretty close to bein' jewelry ore,' he said. 'Know where there's any more of it?'

'Wish I did, if it's that good.' Hashknife laughed. 'I suppose somebody dropped it.'

Steele shook hands with Mrs. Corey and promised to come out again.

'Come out any time,' she urged. 'You are always welcome, Silver.'

'It's good to hear you call me that again,' he said, 'and it will be good to come out here once in a while.'

Hashknife walked out to the horse with Steele.

'I know all about you and your pardner workin' out here for nothin',' he told Hashknife. 'It's shore good of you. And I know about Van Avery bringin' out that load of stuff. Under the circumstances, I can't offer 'em anythin'; but you let me know when they're runnin' short and I'll make a philanthropist out of some of the boys.'

Hashknife promised to let him know, then he went to the bunkhouse, where he sprawled on a bed and blew smoke rings at the ceiling. Was that piece of ore really from that prospect hole, or had some higrader lost it there? He wondered. If Nelson had struck rich ore, why had he quit? Did Payzant examine the prospect and get killed for his curiosity, or was that prospect connected in some way with the killings?

Suddenly an idea struck him, and he sat up abruptly. Slowly, he inhaled a mouthful of smoke, his eyes half-closed. He got to his feet and went back to the stable, where he had left his saddled horse. Taking a small coil of half-inch rope, he rode back to the north line, tied the rope to a piece of the old windlass, and went down to the bottom.

Hashknife knew little about formations, but his eyes were keen. He studied the pitch of the formation, dug out a few pieces with his knife, and crawled back up the rope. One of the pieces, not over half an inch thick, was the same as the piece he had shown Steele.

He coiled up the rope, whistling unmusically between his teeth. Then he rode back to the ranch.

'Where you been?' asked Sleepy, eyeing the coil of rope.

Hashknife tossed the rope around a post and slid from his saddle.

'Packin' a lynch rope?' asked Sleepy.

'Practicin',' said Hashknife.

'You ain't figurin' on lynchin' somebody, are you?'

'Oh, I reckon the law will be sufficient. Ain't it pretty near eatin' time?'

'Pretty near,' replied Sleepy, regarding Hashknife quizzically. 'No use askin' any questions, I don't reckon.'

'Wait'll I git some answers, pardner.'

Silver Steele's visit was the main subject of conversation at the supper-table that evening. It made Gladys very happy to know that Ken's father felt differently about their marriage. In

130

fact, it seemed to lift the depressed spirits of all the family.

Shortly after supper, Gladys went upstairs to write some letters, and Elene asked Hashknife and Sleepy to stay and spend the evening with them in the living-room. There was an old phonograph and a number of well-worn records, which Sleepy proceeded to play. Elene told them of her short stay at a secretarial school in Chicago.

'I think I am glad that is over,' she said. 'A few months in the city was all I could stand.'

'You don't belong there,' Hashknife told her. 'You can't transplant a yucca to a paved street and expect it to do well.'

'Keep the cactus in Arizona,' Elene laughed.

'Yeah, and the roses.'

'Didja ever hear "The Holy City"?' asked Sleepy. He had already played it twice in succession.

'Play "Rancho Grande," ' suggested Elene.

'Oh, yeah. That's the tum-tidy-um Mexican thing. Shore; that's *muy buena musica*. Wait'll I paw it out of this bunch.'

Gladys came softly down the stairs, her eyes serious.

'There's somebody in the patio,' she whispered. 'I saw them from my window. Two men, I think.'

Sleepy stepped away from the phonograph, but Hashknife motioned for him to start it going again. With the phonograph blaring out a military march, Hashknife and Sleepy went to the back door, which opened on the rear porch, or veranda, in the patio. Elene had run to a side window and peered out at the edge of the curtain. She turned and ran quickly to Hashknife and Sleepy.

'Someone on a horse,' she whispered, 'going toward the patio gate.'

Hashknife hesitated, his hand on the latch, his head thrown up, listening.

From out in the patio came a yelp of fright or anger, the crash of a shot, followed by three more shots fired close together, and the snort of a frightened horse.

Hashknife flung the door open. He and Sleepy sprang out into the patio, guns in hand. A gust of wind blew the powder smoke into their nostrils. A horse ran in a circle, clattering over the flags of the patio, and came to a stop near the steps, snorting softly.

It was getting quite dark. Hashknife stepped out and grasped the horse by the bridle. There was enough light to see a man on the ground, trying to get up. Sleepy landed on him none too gently, while Hashknife quickly tied the horse and went to Sleepy's assistance.

The man was gasping and grunting, but they picked him up bodily and carried him into the house. They paused on the steps to hear the drumming of hoofs far off down the road.

'Well, we got one of 'em, anyway,' panted Sleepy.

'Who is it?' asked Elene anxiously.

'Wait'll we git him in to the light,' replied Hashknife.

They carried him in and sprawled him on the floor, where he goggled up at them, his face dusty, his blond hair almost standing on end.

It was Cornelius Van Avery.

They all stood back and looked at him in amazement, while he pumped the air back into his tortured lungs.

'Where in the devil did you come from?' asked Hashknife.

Van Avery took a deep breath and smiled painfully.

'Phoenix,' he whispered huskily. 'Look!'

He opened his mouth and pointed at his teeth.

'Went down and got me a bridge.'

'Oh, and we thought somebody had killed you!' exclaimed Elene.

They helped him to an easy-chair. Elene got him a drink of water.

'What happened out there?' asked Hashknife.

'I don't know. You see, after I left here that day, I—I—well, I was mad about the way I talked. I knew everybody was laughing at me. So that evening I made up my mind. I didn't want anybody to know where I went; so I walked to Red Hill, took a night train to Phoenix, and had a dentist build me a bridge. When I came back this morning, I bought me a horse and saddle in Red Hill. I wanted to surprise you, so I came straight here. I rode in out there, and I thought it was Hashknife and Sleepy beside the porch. It wasn't very light, though. So I said, "Hello, boys."

'Somebody said, "Look out!" and one of them fired a shot almost in my horse's face. Well'—Van Avery rubbed a sore knee—'the man in Red Hill, who sold me that horse, said he'd like to see anything make that horse buck. I wish he had been here a while ago.'

Van Avery looked around at them, a grin on his face.

'Did you miss me?' he asked.

'Blondy, you've upset the whole country,' declared Sleepy.

'Oh, I'm sorry. But I just had to have that bridge. Notice I don't lisp? Wasn't that terrible?'

'Can you forgive me for laughing that day?' asked Elene.

'I certainly can.'

'But who were those two men who shot at you out there?' asked Mrs. Corey anxiously. 'I think that is of more importance right at present.'

'They're gone,' said Hashknife. 'We heard them goin' down the road.'

'Wasn't you scared?' asked Sleepy.

'I didn't have time,' Van Avery smiled. 'Did somebody catch my horse?'

'He's tied up out there.'

'Good; I've still got transportation to Painted Wells.'

'You'll not go to Painted Wells tonight,' declared Elene. 'You stay right here with us.'

'Dear lady,' said Van Avery seriously, 'I hoped you would say that. Honestly, I do not believe I could ride another mile. The person who first conceived the idea of a human being riding a horse did not have me in mind. Somehow I do not fit.'

'Anyway,' said Sleepy, laughing, 'you didn't have any gun to lose this time. Didja ever find the last one you lost?'

'No, but that doesn't matter; I shall get another.'

Mrs. Corey gave Hashknife and Sleepy some extra bedding, and they went out to the bunkhouse to make a bed for Van Avery.

'Another close call, pardner,' said Hashknife. 'They was waitin' for us to come out.'

Sleepy drew down the curtains in the bunkhouse before he lighted the lamp.

'Yeah, and I'm all goose-pimples yet,' he admitted. 'Damn such a place!'

'Do you want to call it quits?'

'I should say not! By golly, now I'm sore!'

CHAPTER VII
A SPREE IN PAINTED WELLS

Hashknife and Sleepy rode to town with Van Avery the next morning. Handsome almost pawed Van Avery off his horse, he was so glad to see him alive and well again. Van Avery explained why he went to Phoenix. Handsome roared with mirth.

'And here we had him all killed off! One mystery solved itself; and if I ain't mistaken, the others will have to do the same if they're ever solved. Doggone, I'm glad to see you, feller.'

'Where's the sheriff?' asked Hashknife.

'Him? Oh, he's on the road to Porcupine, him and Doc Smedley, ridin' in a spring wagon.'

'Somethin' happen in Porcupine?'

'No, not much. A feller accident'ly killed himself. You don't know Bill Neer, do you? He works for Steve McCord. Steve came in this mornin'. It seems that Bill was reloadin' some .45-70 ca'tridges, and one busted up on him, thereby leavin' him playin' a harp on a damp cloud.'

'How the devil did he do that?' asked Hashknife.

'Experimentin', I reckon. Steve said it seemed that Bill was takin' a bullet out of a ca'tridge, or startin' to. He put the ca'tridge in a vise, and was a-goin' to draw out the bullet with a pair of nippers; but it seems that he accident'ly got the head of the shell into the vise and squeezed down upon her. You know, that'll shoot 'em off.'

'And him standin' in front of it,' said Sleepy. 'That's a sure way to increasin' the angel population.'

'Anyway,' stated Handsome, 'they've gone over to pronounce him dead and bring the body back.'

'Goin' to bury him here?'

'Shore. No preacher in Porcupine nor Red Hill now, and we've got the easiest diggin' graveyard of all three places.'

Van Avery offered to buy a drink, so they all went over to the Yucca Saloon. Ed Ault, behind the bar grunted explosively at sight of Van Avery.

'Where in the world did you come from?' he asked.

'Oh, I just took a little trip,' said Van Avery. 'I really did not intend to upset everyone. You were away, too.'

'I was down at Phoenix,' replied Ault. 'What will you have, gents?'

They named their drinks and Ault proceeded to fill their order.

'I've been in Phoenix,' said Van Avery. 'Nice place. Where do you stay while in Phoenix, Mr. Ault?'

Ault mentioned the biggest hotel in the city.

'I always stay there,' he added.

Hashknife frowned thoughtfully over his drink, wondering why Van Avery should ask that question.

'I see you've got some new teeth,' remarked Ault.

Van Avery laughed.

'I needed them badly. The next time anyone shoots at me, I'm going to keep my mouth shut. At least I can save teeth.'

'Didja shut it last night?' asked Sleepy.

'Lova gosh!' snorted Handsome. 'You wasn't shot at agin, was you?'

The story was told, and Handsome ordered another round of drinks.

'There's a Jonah on this ship,' he declared as he looked upon Van Avery with undisguised amazement. 'Feller, you're hung with horseshoes, don'tcha know it?'

'Bullet-proof,' said Hashknife seriously.

'Ain't that the truth? Who knowed you was back, Blondy?'

'Nobody.'

'But if they was gunnin' for you—'

'They wasn't,' interrupted Hashknife. 'Blondy jist happened to come along at the wrong time for a couple murderin' bushwhackers, who were waitin' for me and Sleepy to come out of the house.'

'Lemme git this straight,' said Handsome. 'Why would a couple bushwhackers be waitin' for you and Sleepy?'

'Scared of us.'

'Scared of you?'

'What have you done to scare anybody?' interjected Ault.

'Prob'ly made faces at somebody,' said Sleepy dryly. 'Some folks are shore touchy thataway. Is that whiskey you're drinkin', Blondy? It is? How long have you been drinkin' whiskey?'

'Since I came to Arizona,' Van Avery answered cockily.

'Uh-huh! That's why your teeth come out easy.'

They laughed and finished their drink, after which they wandered out into the street. Hashknife and Sleepy were going back to the ranch. Van Avery walked over to the horses with them.

'Do you remember the hotel Ault said he patronized in Phoenix?' asked Van Avery.

'Yeah,' nodded Hashknife.

'Well, he didn't,' replied Van Avery. 'I looked through the register, thinking he might have registered there, but I couldn't find his name. I asked the room clerk, and he had never heard of Ault. Then I went to several of the better hotels, but he was not registered at any of them.'

Hashknife adjusted his saddle carefully, finally turning to Van Avery.

'Why didja try to find him in Phoenix?'

'Curiosity,' replied Van Avery seriously.

'Why do you tell me this?'

'I thought you might be curious, too."

'Uh-huh. Well thanks, Blondy. Come out as soon as you can; you're always mighty welcome at the ranch.'

'And don't drink too much of that embalmin' fluid,' advised Sleepy.

Van Avery laughed and waved at them as they went down the street.

Blondy Van Avery was not through drinking for the day. It was a rare thing for Handsome to take more than two or three drinks, but this seemed one of those rare times. He was supposed to stay at the office during the sheriff's absence, which he did—between drinks.

Van Avery insisted on buying all the drinks; and Handsome, who confessed that he never had more than two dollars and six bits at any one time, let Van Avery spend his money freely. But Van Avery shied away from the gambling-tables. He played nickels in the slot machines, but that was as far as he would go on gambling.

It was about supper-time when Handsome confessed to himself that he was drunk. He looked owl-eyed upon Blondy, who had developed a case of stuttering hiccoughs, but who was still steady on his legs.

'I've gug-got to gug-git me a gug-gun,' declared Van Avery.

'Tha's a pious thing for to do,' agreed Handsome. 'Git one with two han'les and we'll both shoot it.'

'Help me pup-pick one out, will you?' asked Van Avery.

Handsome cocked his sombrero over one eye. They went to Nelson's store, where Bush looked upon them with considerable apprehension. This was justified when Van Avery stated that he wanted to buy a new gun—with two handles, if possible.

'We both wan' shoot it,' explained Handsome owlishly.

There were only two guns in stock; a pearl-handled .45 Colt and a cheap, hammerless .32, commonly known as a suicide gun. After thirty minutes of argument over 'muzzle v'locity' and 'pen'tration,' Van Avery took the .45. He had a belt full of ammunition in his room; so they wended their erratic way up to the room, and later appeared on the street, Van Avery wearing his new gun, fully loaded, in its hand-tooled leather holster.

'Th' s'prisin' thing to me is that you can keep your feet,' said Handsome.

'They're fuf-fastened on,' explained Van Avery, after which they went into gales of laughter and hammered each other on the back.

They went back to the Yucca, where the bartender looked upon them with dread, especially when Van Avery insisted on taking out his gun and having Handsome explain its mechanics.

Ault had left the saloon, and no one was there except the bartender and his two jovial customers.

'You can't shoot thish gun, 'less you pull the trigger,' explained Handsome.

'Have to pup-pull it?' queried Van Avery. 'Couldn' you juj-jerk it?'

'You'd mish the targ't.'

'I'd what?'

'Mish.'

'You shound like you losh a tut-tooth, Handsome.'

'Oh, whash use? You never hit nothin'. You couldn't hit that wall back there.'

Bang! The bullet tore through a framed advertising picture, bored a hole through the wall, and probably went off across country. Van Avery staggered back, holding the gun in both hands, while the bartender, thankful to be alive, sprinted out through the rear door.

'Well,' said Handsome critically, 'I admit I'm wrong, Blondy. You did hit the wall. And you alsho chased the barten'er away. Tha's hard luck, 'cause I'm thirshty.'

'That's easy to fuf-fix,' gurgled Van Avery; he proceeded to go behind the bar.

Clumsily he slid out glasses and a bottle. Handsome was about to the point where another straw would break the camel's back. He drank another glass of liquor, looked upon the world with unseeing eyes and swung around with his back to the bar.

Van Avery did not drink this time. There was a six-shooter on a little shelf under the bar, and he picked it up. He looked at Handsome, who was wavering on his legs, shoved the gun inside his belt and went wobbling around the end of the bar.

'Wanna shing,' declared Handsome sleepily.

Van Avery took him by the arm, and they went across the street like a pair of tugboats on a stormy sea.

They stumbled into the sheriff's office. Handsome sprawled full length on a cot and began to snore lustily. Van Avery sat down in the sheriff's chair, shut one eye and looked around the room. With a drunken scowl at the big safe in the corner, he got to his feet and went over to Handsome.

It was after dark when the sheriff and coroner got back to town with the body of Bill Neer. It had been a hard day's work. The sheriff was in bad spirits. Handsome was snoring on the cot, and the sheriff looked him over with a practiced eye. He recognized the symptoms. The doctor had driven on down to his office with the body.

The sheriff stepped back in the jail and asked Ken if he had been fed. Ken hadn't; in fact, he wanted to know whether they were trying to starve him to death.

'Handsome's drunk as a shepherd,' said Banty disgustedly. 'He's a sweet specimen to leave in charge of anythin'.'

The sheriff went back to the office and found Ault there.

'Your deputy kinda fell off the wagon today, didn't he?' accused Ault. 'I don't like to put up a howl, but Handsome and that damn Van Avery shot a hole in my saloon wall, chased my bartender out of the place, and helped themselves.'

'Van Avery? You don't mean the kid that—'

'Didn't you know he came back today? He'd been away some place to get his teeth fixed.'

'Well, darn his hide! So he came back.'

'And shot up my place,' grunted Ault.

The sheriff shook his head wearily.

'I dunno. I guess it don't pay me to go away for the day. Wasn't any damage done, was there?'

'Just a hole in the wall and a scared bartender.'

'That Van Avery beats hell,' sighed the sheriff. 'Where is he?'

'Gone to bed at the hotel. The last anybody heard of him, he was tryin' to sing "The Dyin' Cowboy."'

Ault went back to the Yucca, and the sheriff proceeded to eat a meal and bring one to Ken. About two hours later, as the sheriff was preparing for bed, Doc Smedley came up to the office.

'Did you see Hartley?' he asked.

'No, I ain't seen him,' replied the sheriff. 'Is he in town?'

'He was down at my office when I got there. Asked me as a personal favor to dig the bullet out of Neer. I didn't want to do it, but he—he's a hard fellow to refuse. I said it didn't mean a thing, because Neer was killed accidentally; but he said somethin' about making a collection of bullets that killed folks in a queer way.'

'Well, didja git it for him?'

'Wasn't any harm in it, was there, Banty?'

'Not if you was willin' to go to that trouble, Doc.'

'Sure, I gave it to him. He said he didn't mind if I told you, but he said to not tell anybody else.'

'He's a queer jigger, Doc. What in hell would he want of that bullet? We've got plenty evidence how Neer was killed.'

'He said somethin' about a collection of bullets.'

'That might be, Doc; some folks collect damn funny things.'

'Well, I just wanted you to know about it.'

'That's fine. Good night.'

As the doctor turned to the door, Ault came in. He knew Bill Neer, and he wanted to know what arrangements had been made for the funeral.

'Goin' to bury him tomorrow, I suppose,' said the sheriff. 'Steve said he'd be over.'

'Killed instantly, wasn't he?' asked Ault.

'Well, he didn't live long,' replied the doctor. 'That big bullet didn't have so much penetration, but enough to do the job. It wasn't battered up much.'

'Did you dig it out?' asked Ault, rather perturbed.

'As a favor,' said the doctor. 'Hashknife Hartley said he was making a collection of bullets that kill folks in queer ways, and he wanted this one.'

For the next few days Hashknife and Sleepy stayed at the Corey ranch. They had the place in good shape by this time, but Hashknife knew that things were such as to make them marked men now. He had no definite evidence against anyone—no jury evidence—although he was satisfied that he was on the right track.

The sheriff came out with Silver Steele. Bill Neer had been buried, the surgeon from Phoenix was attending Judge Frazer, and Perry Donlin, of Yuma, was in town, trying to prepare a defense for Ken Steele.

'But he's scared to death,' declared Silver Steele, speaking of the new attorney. 'He wouldn't have time to prepare a good defense, if he wasn't afraid. I can't convince him that he won't get shot on the first day of the trial, which is day after tomorrow.'

'And I found out who was with Ken the night before the murder of Milt Corey,' said the sheriff.

'Mark Hawker was with him, and so was Brad Thatcher. Mark told me that they was all drunk. Ken got sore at Ed Ault and was goin' to shoot him; so Mark took the gun away from him. They was havin' a great time, and Mark says he tried to pawn the gun in a saloon for a round of drinks. But he says Ken got the gun back. If anybody else got the gun, Mark don't know about it.'

'Did you find out if Brad Thatcher was in town the mornin' after?' asked Hashknife.

'Mark didn't know. I asked Ault and he said Thatcher left about midnight.'

'Well, that don't help much,' admitted Hashknife. 'How is Frazer gettin' along?'

'Still unconscious. Pretty tough case, I reckon.'

'Is Van Avery still in town?' asked Sleepy.

'That pest!' The sheriff snorted. 'You heard about him and Handsome gettin' drunk, didn't you? Ran the bartender out of the Yucca and done their own bartendin'.'

'No!' exclaimed Hashknife.

'Shore did. Van Avery shot a hole in the wall, and the bartender pulled his freight. I don't savvy Van Avery. You can't faze the danged fool. Packin' a big gun on his hip, and he says the next man that takes a shot at him is goin' to git leaded up plenty. When he came to Painted Wells, he talked like a dictionary. Now he's learnin' to cuss and talk like a cowpuncher.'

'I don't savvy him,' said Steele. 'He asked me

yesterday if I was sure that my caretakers wasn't higradin' on me up at the mine.'

'Well, are you?' asked Hashknife seriously.

'Ortelle is a reliable man,' replied Steele stiffly.

'Uh-huh; but you must remember that somebody loaded that gun for Ryan.'

'I know it, Hartley; and it worries me all the time.'

Van Avery came out late that afternoon, all dressed up in his ornamented chaps, big hat and big gun. They were all glad to see him.

'Watch me,' Van Avery chuckled. 'Someday I'll be mayor of Painted Wells. Handsome wants me to run for sheriff at the next election.'

'Goin' to stick around and grow up with the country, eh?' laughed Hashknife.

'I am not; I'm going to stick around and give the country a chance to catch up with me. I'm the little angel child that got drunk the other day and shot up the Yucca. Fact. I drank Handsome under the table. But, oh, wasn't I sick? Never again.'

'You have changed,' said Elene.

'Yes, I have, Miss Corey. And I'm going to keep on changing until you folks are willing to accept me as one of you. I'm here to stay.'

'Why?' asked Gladys Steele, rather amused at him.

'Because I like it. Folks are real out here; shoot at you and everything. Isn't that right, Mrs. Corey?'

'Well, bless your heart, I suppose it is,' said Mrs. Corey, laughing. 'They certainly shot at you.'

'That's over,' he said severely. 'I've been out practicing on tin cans. My latest score is two tomatoes and one corn out of ten shots. Yesterday I got me a couple of condensed milk, shooting with both hands.'

'Why not get a shotgun?' asked Sleepy.

'Nope; I'm a good sport. Give everybody an even break.'

'Well, don't lose your gun,' advised Hashknife dryly.

'Not me. Next time my horse starts bucking, I'm going to throw my gun in the road where I can find it easy. He hasn't bucked since the other night in the patio, but he seems to be figuring on something all the time. Talk about the glorious uncertainty. Mrs. Corey, am I invited to supper?'

'You certainly are, Mr. Van Avery.'

'Call me Blondy. I tell you I'm goin' Arizona.'

'Spoken like a cowpoke.' Sleepy laughed. 'Stick with it long enough and we'll understand what you mean when you ask for water.'

'That stuff!'

'You'll like it when you grow up,' said Hashknife.

Van Avery took off his chaps and sat down in the patio with Elene.

'I don't lisp,' he told her seriously, 'so don't laugh at me if I repeat what I said the last time you saw me with two teeth out.'

'It wasn't what you said—it was the way you said it.'

'Gee, that sure takes a load off my mind,' said Van Avery fervently. 'You see, I am going to stay in this country. I've lived in a city all my life, and all I know of the West is what I have read. Now I want to stay here.'

'And raise cattle?' asked Elene.

'No, I believe I'd rather go in for mining. But that is in the future. I'd rather talk about you. Are you going back to study again?'

Elene shook her head.

'That is impossible now.'

'I'm rather glad about that. You would be somebody's stenographer for a long time; and if you were lucky you might, in time, become a private secretary for some crabbed old financier. And you'd barely make a living. Do you know what I think is the finest career for a woman?'

'What is that?' asked Elene.

'Marriage.'

'I suppose you read that in a book.'

'I did, but I agree with it thoroughly.'

'What do you know about marriage?' Elene laughed. 'Have you any ideas on the subject?'

'The biggest idea in the world. You remember what I lisped to you that night?'

'Marriage,' said Elene, 'is a serious thing.'

'Oh, gee!' sighed Van Avery. 'All the way out here I rehearsed what I was going to say to you. I said it over and over to the horse until I had it just right. Now I can't remember a word of it. Marriage may be a serious thing; but the things that lead up to one are more serious to me. You see, I never made love to a girl before.'

'Are you making love to me, Blondy?' asked Elene.

'I guess not,' he replied soberly. 'I'm so darned dumb.'

'I'm glad,' said Elene simply.

'You're glad I'm dumb?'

'No, glad you are not making love to me.'

Before Van Avery could think of a reply, Gladys came out on the porch. She saw them and started to leave, but Van Avery halted her.

'Mrs. Steele,' he said seriously, 'what did your husband say to you when he asked you to marry him?'

Gladys hesitated over her reply, looking at Van Avery curiously.

'Why, he just asked me to marry him.'

'Just like that?'

'Why, yes. Were you'—she glanced side-wise at Elene—'were you thinking of asking my sister to marry you?'

'Not merely thinking—I was positive,' replied Van Avery.

'Excuse me,' said Gladys. She went quickly inside the house.

Van Avery looked at Elene.

'Didn't sound very romantic, did it?' he asked.

'What was that?'

'The way Ken Steele proposed to your sister. Of course, it condenses things; puts the whole thing in one sentence. Suppose Romeo had said the same thing to Juliet. But, looking at it from another angle, you understand I am not a Romeo. Gee, if I could only remember what I said to that horse.'

Elene laughed with him.

'Let's forget the marriage idea,' she said. 'I haven't any idea of marrying anybody. You don't know a thing about me, and I'm sure I know nothing about you.'

'Tell me something,' said Van Avery softly. 'Is there anybody else, Elene; anybody you might be thinking about?'

'I told you I wasn't thinking about marrying anybody.'

'Fine. I mean, I'm glad you aren't thinking of marrying anybody else. How old are you, Elene?'

'Are you in the habit of asking questions like that, Blondy?'

'Oh, shucks! Excuse it, please. That's just another of my dumb breaks. I wish I could do the right thing at the right time.'

'Go wash your face,' yelled Sleepy from the patio gate. 'It's time to eat.'

'That's my chance!' exclaimed Van Avery. 'It's funny how my wish came true.'

It was after dark when they finished supper. Van Avery wanted to start back to Painted Wells, but the Coreys wanted him to stay all night at the ranch.

'You're not goin' back tonight,' declared Hashknife. 'Any time you travel the roads, travel 'em in daylight.'

During the general discussion, Hashknife slipped out, untied Van Avery's horse, and led it out of the patio to the stable. The barn door was wide open, and Hashknife stepped in boldly. There was not a sound of any kind, but his intuition told him he had made a mistake. But before he could move something crashed down upon his head, and he went sprawling, unconscious. The horse backed away, snorting softly, as two men came out, carrying Hashknife between them. One of them chuckled softly as he said:

'Hell, this is better than I expected. Shot at a gopher and hit a fox.'

They carried Hashknife about a hundred feet from the stable, where they proceeded to truss him on the back of a horse and twist a gag between his teeth. They rode away in the darkness.

It was probably fifteen minutes before Hash-knife's absence was noticed. Sleepy went to the bunkhouse, but it was in darkness. Van Avery's horse was gone; but when Sleepy ran down to the stable, he found the horse near the corral fence. The stable door was open, but Sleepy did not go in. He called Hashknife's name. There was no response. Van Avery called from the house, and came down to the stable. Together they went into the stable and lighted the lantern.

'Where do you suppose he can be?' asked Van Avery anxiously.

Sleepy's face was pale in the lantern-light.

'Lord only knows, Blondy. I'm scared. He prob'ly tried to stable your bronc, and they was layin' for him. I'm—'

Sleepy swung the lantern low along the entrance, dropped on one knee, and swept up a black-handled six-shooter.

'Damn 'em, they've got him!' he grunted. 'Here's his gun!'

Sleepy leaned back against the wall, gripping the gun in his hand.

'They bushed him,' he said huskily. 'Knocked him down and the gun slipped out of the holster. They worked in the dark—didn't see the gun. I ain't got brains enough to even think where to look for him.'

They went back to the ranch-house. Sleepy sank down in a chair, while Van Avery tried to tell them what had happened. The Coreys tried to tell Sleepy that Hashknife was all right; that everything would turn out right. But Sleepy was not convinced.

'I've got to do somethin',' he muttered. 'Got to stop 'em. You folks don't understand. Hashknife's smarter than all of 'em. He'd hang the whole gang, and they know it. That's why they got him. Do you think they'd hesitate to kill him?'

'Who are they, Sleepy?' asked Elene. 'Don't you know whom he suspects?'

'You never know who he suspects,' replied Sleepy miserably. 'He never tells anybody—not even me.'

Sleepy got to his feet.

'I'm goin' to town,' he said. 'I've got to do somethin'.'

'But you can't do anything, Sleepy,' said Elene. 'You don't even know who it is nor which way they took him. Stay here until morning.'

'He wouldn't, if it was me. I've got to go.'

'I'll go with you,' declared Van Avery, but Sleepy shook his head.

'You stay here, Blondy. Thank you jist the same, but I'll go alone.'

They sat there together in the living-room, and heard the rattle of hoofs as Sleepy galloped down the dark road to Painted Wells.

Van Avery shook his head sadly.

'If they've killed Hashknife Hartley, it will be a sad day for the folks around here,' he said.

'What do you mean?' asked Elene.

'You don't know it, but Hartley is the smartest range detective in the country.'

'Range detective? Why, I didn't know that. Did he tell you?'

'He never tells anything,' replied Van Avery. 'I found it out in Phoenix.'

CHAPTER VIII
BANK LOOT

When Hashknife regained consciousness, he was still roped to the horse, but he was too sick and groggy to care much about anything. He had been hit a terrific blow which had nearly finished him, and he did not realize much of anything until after he had been taken off the horse. There was no strength in his body, and a hammer seemed to be beating on the back of his head. He heard voices, but they were far away, and he was not interested in what they were saying. He wanted a drink of water, but the gag prevented him from asking for one.

They were half-dragging him along now. He seemed to feel his feet bumping over obstructions but he was unable to lift them up. Then the atmosphere changed suddenly, and he could dimly see wavering lights which might be candles. It smelled musty. There was a sort of booming sound as they went along, and his brain registered the splash of water. The bumping of his feet was regular now, as if over the rungs of a ladder.

Finally they stopped, and the men seemed to be holding a consultation. It was something about somebody being almost dead, and about ropes being left. He was lying flat on the wet ground now, and he could see the flicker of light against wet rocks.

Then the lights went away, and he could hear the booming sound again. The cold water revived him a little. He tried to figure out what he was doing there. There was no gag now, and he managed to get his lips against a trickle of water. How good that water tasted! As it dripped on his aching head, his brain began to clear.

Suddenly there was a thudding explosion, which helped to shake him from his lethargy. He could move his arms and legs, but his head seemed to weigh a ton. It was so dark that he could not see an inch; a clammy darkness with dripping water.

He became cognizant of his surroundings, reached out and found a damp, dripping rock wall on each side of him. No, there was no wall on one side—not within reach. A light! That was what he needed. He found some matches in his pocket and, after some difficulty, he scratched one. In the flare of the match he realized that he was at the end of a tunnel. Not a big tunnel—more like the tunnel a prospector of small means would make.

The match flared out, and Hashknife leaned against the wall. His head was getting better now. Why was he in this place? He didn't remember being in a place like this before. A tunnel meant a mine. Into his brain flashed the name—Comanche Chief. He sat up and held his head in his hands. He remembered everything now. That blow in the dark. It seemed as if it had happened years ago, but he knew that it was not long since. His head was bleeding a little.

Digging out another match, he scratched it carefully. Almost at his feet was the stump of a miner's candle, four or five inches long. With trembling fingers he managed to light it and take stock of himself. His holster was empty, his clothes torn. But he was not tied. There was an odor of dynamite fumes in the air, which seemed to be getting stronger all the time.

After a supreme effort he managed to get to his feet, holding to the wall for support. When the dizziness passed, he took the candle and moved cautiously down the narrow drift. There was a wooden car track, warped and twisted. Then Hashknife realized that the place was an old abandoned tunnel.

The powder fumes as he advanced down the tunnel almost nauseated him. The passageway seemed very long, but his eyes did not pick up the welcome sight of the tunnel mouth. He stumbled weakly up against some dirt rubble, where his candle told him the story. There were the twisted broken timbers and the loose, broken rock. He knew now what had happened.

For a distance the old tunnel had been timbered before striking the solid formation, and it had fallen in, imprisoning him under the earth. He remembered that explosion now. They had untied him, left him there to die; and if the old tunnel were ever reopened there would be no evidences of murder.

There was no use trying to dig out. One glance was sufficient to convince him that it could not be done, especially with bare hands. He sat down on a rock and considered his plight. He had been in many tough spots in his life, but in nothing like this. No one would ever look for him in such a place; and even if they did, it would be after every other place had been searched, and he would be dead long before that.

There was no use going back to the face of the drift. That would only put him deeper under the earth. He looked at the candle and wondered how long it would burn. Not long. It had already burned an inch. He wondered if he should conserve it.

'Shucks,' he decided, 'might as well shoot the works. Mebbe I can find another piece of candle.'

He plodded painfully all the way back to the face of the drift, but there were no more pieces of candle; so he came back and sat down on the rock. Hashknife's optimism had vanished. His head was thumping, and he attributed it to the powder fumes. Powder fumes? They didn't seem as bad as they were. In fact, he could hardly smell them; and he wondered if it were merely because he had become used to them.

He held his candle up nearer the roof. There did not seem to be much smoke; not nearly so much as there had been. A trickle of water snuffed his precious candle and, as he dried the wick on his shirt, he happened to glance upward.

For several moments he did not move.

'It can't be,' he whispered. 'No such luck. My God, it is, jist as sure as fate!'

With trembling hands he lighted the candle, then snuffed it. Over his head, up through that mass of broken rock was a star—a single star, twinkling! Hashknife was laughing now. He was still light-headed, but he knew he was not mistaken. He lighted the candle and stuck it on a piece of broken timber. With his two hands he ripped up a fifteen-foot section of that old two-by-four car rail and carefully shoved it up against that tiny fissure, blotting out the star. Gravel and dirt rattled down along the rail as he slowly worked it farther out. A large piece of rock narrowly missed his head, but he kept working. A stream of gravel buried his candle, but he did not mind. He could see more stars now. A few more pokes, a cascade of rock and gravel—the hole was two feet across now.

Panting heavily, he sat down and pawed gravel until he sifted out the stump of his candle, which he managed to light again. He needed that illumination now, because a mistake in climbing out through that hole might throw him back into the tunnel and cause a slide which would bury him forever.

After a long rest, and using the old rail as a sort of makeshift ladder, he began his climb. Uninjured, it would have been no task for him; but his arms were weak and the pain in his head nearly blinded him. In fact, he did not remember getting out; but there he was, lying on his back, his feet dangling in the hole.

It was moonlight. Just behind him was a scraggly old tree, its shadow strongly etched on the ground beside him; and that shadow seemed to be moving slowly. Was it imagination? Hashknife instinctively swung his feet around and crawled blindly away. He heard the sound of earth caving, the snapping of branches, and when he looked back there was only the top of the tree visible. The hole where he had come out was sealed up. The cave-in was complete.

After a considerable time he was able to investigate a little. The tunnel had been driven into the foot of a hill where the slope was slight. From the cave-in where the timbering ended to the mouth of the tunnel was about thirty feet, and in that distance it had only gained a perpendicular depth of possibly eight feet. That fact had been Hashknife's salvation.

He found a trail at the mouth of the tunnel and followed it. He had no idea where he was. The pain in his head was not so bad now, and he was getting stronger. Around the point of a hill he came to a stop. Off to his left and farther up the hill were the big buildings of the Comanche Chief. The black bulk of the old stamp mill was strongly etched against the moonlit sky; but as far as Hashknife could see, there were no lights.

He knew where he was now. This trail would intersect with the road to the Comanche Chief. He plodded along and struck the dusty road. Down in the valley he could see the lights of Painted Wells. Should he go down there? He stopped and tried to think what would be the best thing to do. He could get a horse down there. It was at least four miles to the Diamond C ranch—a long walk in his present condition.

Finally he laughed harshly and looked up at the moon.

'I'm a dead man,' he said aloud. 'They can go and take a look at that cave-in, and it'll prove I'm still in there. So I reckon I'll stay dead awhile and see how they like it.'

And he went stumbling down the road.

Sleepy Stevens had cooled down a little by the time he reached town. He realized that there was little to be done until some plan of action had been worked out. He found Handsome in the office and told him what had happened. Handsome hunted up the sheriff, who freely admitted that he hadn't any ideas. Handsome had one comforting suggestion.

'If they was a-goin' to kill him, why didn't they? A feller has always got a chance to git away if he's jist kidnaped.'

Sleepy agreed that this was possible: but he was doubtful that any of that bad bunch would ever give Hashknife a chance to escape.

'You go back and go to bed,' advised the sheriff. 'We'll be out there by daylight and see if there's any chance to foller 'em.'

Sleepy agreed, but he went over to the Yucca Saloon. He wanted to see who was there and who might come in. Ault spoke pleasantly to him, but Sleepy was in no mood to be pleasant. He sat down and appeared to watch the play in a poker game, but all the time his mind was trying to figure out where to look for his partner.

If Hashknife had only told him some of his suspicions! But all was a blank to Sleepy. For over an hour he sat there, the loneliest person in the world. The lure of the distant hills was gone now. He would never ride over them again, alone. Probably settle down and use a hoe.

He got up and wandered around the town, looking at everyone he met; and finally he went back to the Yucca and sat down again.

'I ain't got any brains,' he told himself. 'All I'm good for is to ride and shoot. Be all right, if I knowed where to ride and who to shoot.'

'Your pardner didn't come in with you tonight?' asked Ault.

Sleepy shook his head. He didn't want to talk to anybody; just sit there and think. Ault watched him curiously, wondering why this unsmiling cowpuncher sat there hour after hour.

It was two o'clock in the morning when Sleepy walked from the Yucca, mounted his horse, and rode slowly back to the ranch. He was not afraid of an ambush. In fact, he wished somebody would ambush him. He wanted action.

There was no light at the ranch-house. He stabled his horse and went up to the bunkhouse. He lighted the old lamp and sat down at the table to roll a smoke, not wanting to go to bed.

'Why don'tcha go to bed, you damned owl?'

Sleepy jumped to his feet so quickly that he struck the table and knocked the chimney off the lamp. Sitting up in a bunk, his head bandaged with a towel, was Hashknife Hartley. He looked like a Hindu. Sleepy recovered his balance and stared at Hashknife.

'Where you been?' he asked huskily.

'Gittin' myself killed,' Hashknife answered dryly.

Sleepy came over closer.

'Yeah? They failed agin, eh?'

'No,' replied Hashknife seriously, 'they made good this time.'

Sleepy's glance roved around the bunkhouse.

'Where's Blondy?' he asked.

'He wasn't here when I got back. I reckon they had him sleep in the house. Where have you been?'

'Aw, f'r Pete's sake!' blurted Sleepy. 'I've been to Painted Wells tryin' to figure out where to find you. Are you all right? What's all that bandage for?'

'Keepin' my brains in.' Hashknife grinned. 'Gimme them papers and some Durham; I'm about to tell you the story of my life, pardner.'

After his cigarette was lighted, Hashknife proceeded to tell Sleepy what had happened to him, after which Sleepy removed the bandage and put on a fresh one. The cut was not bad, but there was plenty of swelling yet, and his head still ached. He had blisters on his feet from the long walk, and many bruises on his body from rough handling.

'Can you do a rough job of actin'?' asked Hashknife.

'What kind of actin'?'

'I'm goin' to remain dead awhile, Sleepy. You say the sheriff is comin' out here early? All right. We've got to let the Coreys in on this, but not Van Avery. Git him out of the house early. There's a cellar under the house where I'll hide out. Don't let another soul know I ever came back. Help 'em hunt for me. Cry if you feel like it.'

'Hell, I wouldn't cry over you, you long-legged kangaroo.'

'Do your own actin'.' Hashknife grinned. 'But git Van Avery out of the house and give me a chance to tell Ma Corey what I want done.'

'All right.'

'Glad I came back?'

'Yeah—shore. You lost me a lot of good sleep, dang you.'

'Prob'ly lose you more, too. Jist remember, you're takin' orders from a ghost, Sleepy.'

'That'll make me a medium, won't it?'

'You'll never be medium, Sleepy; you're too hard-boiled.'

There was not an overflow crowd at the opening of Ken Steele's trial. That would come later as many did not care to sit through the selection of the jury. Perry Donlin, Ken's attorney, admitted to Silver Steele that he had little on which to base his defense. Ken's story was all he had.

On the other hand, about all the prosecution had was Ken's gun. But the prosecuting attorney was satisfied that this one bit of evidence would be plenty. Marked Exhibit A, it was on the clerk's desk when the trial opened; and during the first recess Donlin asked to see the gun.

The prosecuting attorney took it from its wrappings and placed in on the table. The initials were carved on the right side of the butt plate, and Donlin scrutinized them closely. He looked quizzically at the prosecutor and asked him what Ken's initials were.

'K. G. S.,' replied the prosecutor.

'That's mighty queer,' said Donlin. 'The initials on this gun are E. J. A.'

The prosecutor grabbed the gun and looked at the initials. He turned the gun over in his hands and spun the cylinder. The gun was a .44 Colt, fully loaded. Ken's gun was a .45 Colt, one cartridge having been fired.

The prosecutor swallowed heavily.

'Where's the sheriff?' he asked hoarsely. 'Bring him in here.'

The sheriff looked blankly at the gun, not understanding what the prosecutor was talking about. Finally he said—

'It was in that package?'

'I unwrapped it myself!' snapped the prosecutor.

'That's the package that was in my safe.' They glared at each other, and were still glaring at each other when the judge came back from his chambers.

'Those are Ed Ault's initials,' said the sheriff.

'They're not Ken Steele's!' snapped the prosecutor.

'That's the only gun in my safe.'

'Gentlemen,' said Donlin, 'it seems that we are deadlocked.'

The prosecutor turned to the judge.

'Your Honor, the main exhibit in this case, consisting of a revolver found at the scene of the crime, and bearing the initials of Ken Steele, was labeled and locked in the sheriff's safe. We have just unwrapped the exhibit and we find an entirely different gun with different initials.'

He handed the gun to the judge, who examined it.

'Whose initials are these?' asked the judge.

'Ed Ault, the owner of the Yucca Saloon,' replied the sheriff.

'Is Mr. Ault in the courtroom? If not, bring him here.'

Handsome came in with Ken; and almost at the same time, Ken's wife, Mrs. Corey, and Elene came in, Van Avery following them. It did not require much time for the sheriff to find Ed Ault. The gambler was a little nervous, as the sheriff had not told him why the judge wished to see him.

'Your initials are E. J. A.?' asked the judge.

Ault nodded quickly.

'Yes, Judge.'

'Is this your gun?'

Ault took the gun which the judge handed him.

'That's my gun,' he said. 'Where—who brought it here?'

The judge looked keenly at the sheriff.

'You have had charge of this gun since the day of the murder, Sheriff. Who else has access to your safe?'

'My deputy. C'mere, Handsome.'

'What's wrong with the gun?' asked Handsome.

'Anybody had your keys to the safe?' asked the sheriff.

'They shore ain't!' Handsome dug in his pocket and took out the key. 'She's been right in my pocket all the time.'

The judge rubbed his chin thoughtfully, while the rest of the group shifted uneasily. The prosecutor was furious.

'Have you a transcript of the preliminary hearing?' asked the judge, and the prosecutor hurried to give him a copy, which the judge perused with aggravating slowness. Finally he shoved it aside.

'According to this,' he said slowly, 'the gun is not fully described. It merely says a Colt revolver, bearing the initials K. G. S. It does not state just where those initials are on the gun, nor does it state model or caliber. And it also appears that the prisoner did not identify it as being his property.'

'He refused to talk,' blurted the prosecutor. 'At the coroner's inquest he refused to say anything. Others identified it as his gun. Why, it had his initials on the handle. The sheriff has either been willfully or ignorantly negligent in his duties, and I—'

'And that's about all out of you, feller!' snapped the sheriff.

There was no one acting as bailiff; so the judge hammered on his desk and demanded order. The Corey family and Ken Steele did not know what it was all about. Silver Steele, seated halfway back in the room, got to his feet.

'Gentlemen!' snapped the judge. 'This is no place for a brawl. Does the prosecution desire to proceed with the trial?'

Glaring around at the excited crowd, the prosecutor turned to the judge.

'Under the circumstances, the State is not prepared to continue the case. With our evidence stolen, or carelessly misplaced, I would ask that the charge be dismissed and the case closed.'

The judge nodded curtly and ordered it so made of record.

Ken Steele was in a daze. Mrs. Corey was crying, and Van Avery was trying to organize a cheering section to give a yell for the prosecuting attorney. Ault hurried from the courtroom and went back to the saloon, where he looked under the bar.

'Where's my gun?' he asked the bartender.

'You took it, didn't you?' replied the drink-dispenser.

'Oh, hell!' Ault snorted and walked away.

The sheriff and deputy were as much at sea as anybody. Silver Steele shook hands with Ken and the Corey family, while Donlin stood around, hands shoved down in his pockets, enjoying it hugely. It was the easiest case he had ever won; and he was not even interested to know who had made the substitution. His client was free.

'Yeah, I'm free,' said Ken. 'That's worth a lot; but I haven't been proved innocent.'

'You got an even break,' responded Handsome. 'They didn't prove you guilty.'

Ken took his wife back to the ranch. Silver Steele rode with Mrs. Corey and Elene. Van Avery wanted to do something particularly devilish; so he went over to the Yucca and bought three quarts of champagne. He put them under his arm and went down to the sheriff's office. They had been in a glass case on the back bar for several months, possibly years. Van Avery never stopped to think that the stuff should be chilled.

Handsome was alone in the office, examining the lock of the safe. He looked at the gold-topped bottles, kicked the safe shut, and lost all interest in it.

'Whatcha got, Blondy?' he asked.

'Bubble juice, Handsome. Didn't you ever drink champagne?'

'Horned toads! Champagne? How much did them cost you, feller?'

'Thirty dollars. Where's the sheriff?'

'Prob'ly arguin' with somebody. He's sore, don'tcha know it? Betcha he knocks hell out of a certain lawyer before sundown. Need a corkscrew, don'tcha?'

Van Avery eyed the bottles. He had never opened one in his life. He had a corkscrew on his pocketknife.

'How about a couple cups?' asked Handsome. 'I'll get 'em.'

Van Avery sat down in the sheriff's chair and proceeded to loosen the wires on a bottle, while Handsome went into a back room to find the cups. Someone came into the office, and Van Avery glanced up. It was the prosecuting attorney, red-faced, breathing heavily. He came in close to Van Avery.

'Where is the sheriff?' he demanded hotly.

'You really should cool down,' advised Van Avery, twisting a blade in the wires.

'Cool down! I'll cool somebody down before I'm through. Of all the asinine, blundering, incompetent—'

Whap! With a report like a pistol-shot the cork blasted out of that bottle of lukewarm, badly shaken champagne, and it hit the prosecuting attorney square in the nose. The contents of the bottle seemed to leap upon him, the bulk of it striking the middle of his chest.

The surprise impact sent the lawyer reeling back, grasping at his nose, while Van Avery leaned back, blinking his amazement at the empty bottle.

Handsome had returned in time to see what happened, and he doubled up with glee. Van Avery's right hand shot out and grasped another bottle. But the prosecutor did not wait for a second assault; he went out and headed across the street, mopping his face.

'That ain't the way to open 'em,' suggested Handsome.

'I got it all the way open, didn't I?' asked Van Avery. 'What do you suppose they put in this stuff—dynamite?'

'You hold down the cork,' explained Handsome. 'Lemme show you. Boy, what you done to that law gent was plenty.'

They looked at each other and laughed heartily.

'He'll prob'ly swear out a warrant and have you arrested for assault,' chuckled Handsome, as he took the bottle and began his demonstration. He held his thumb over the cork and cut the wires.

'Git the cups, Blondy; this stuff is ready.'

Squee-e-e-e-bung! The cork rebounded from the ceiling. Handsome tried to keep his broad thumb over the neck of the bottle, which only caused the liquor to squirt at right angles all over him. Van Avery dodged and sneaked behind the desk until the spraying was over.

Then Van Avery stood up and considered the

dripping Handsome, who was mopping champagne out of his eyes.

'Well,' said Van Avery dryly, 'thus endeth
twenty dollars' worth of squirts. I've heard of
champagne baths, but these two are the first I
have ever seen. Let's tie a tail on that other one
and call it a skyrocket.'

Cautiously Handsome shoved the full bottle
back on the desk, eyeing it closely as though
fearing an explosion. Then he leaned back and
looked at Van Avery.

'My Lord, supposin' you had that stuff inside
you and it started actin' up thataway!'

'It would be an awful strain,' admitted
Van Avery dryly.

'Take a man to stand it,' grunted the deputy.
'I tell you what we better do—me and you,
Blondy.'

'What?'

'Sneak out careful-like, go across the street and
drink somethin' docile.'

'All right. But darn it, I wanted to celebrate
right, Handsome.'

'I appreciate that fact; but next time git somethin' you can hook a fuse onto.'

Van Avery took a sheet of paper, wrote on it,
'Compliments of an Admirer to the Sheriff,'
and fastened it to the remaining bottle. Then he
and Handsome went across the street to get, as
Handsome said, something docile.

Ed Ault was at the bar. He accepted Van Avery's invitation to drink with them, because he wanted to see what Handsome thought about that stolen gun. In answer to his query, Handsome countered with—

'When did you lose that gun, Ed?'

'I never lost it; somebody stole it.'

'When?'

'I dunno. You don't think for a moment that I unlocked your safe and switched guns, do you?'

'Ed, I'm all through thinkin',' stated the deputy.

'Any news of Hartley?' asked Ault.

Handsome shook his head.

'I wish there was.'

'What does his partner think about it?'

'Sleepy? Oh, he jist goes around kinda dumb. Hell, I shore feel sorry for Sleepy.'

'I feel sorry for the whole country,' said Van Avery seriously.

'Why?' asked Ault.

'Because if Hartley had stayed, he'd probably have hung a lot of murderers around here.'

'How do you figure that?'

'Merely my opinion. The whole trouble is, Hartley never talked. If he had told what he knew, somebody might have carried out his schemes.'

'Meanin' that Hartley was a detective?'

'That was his reputation. I'll buy another drink. How is Frazer, the lawyer, coming along?'

'Still alive,' grunted Handsome, reaching for the bottle.

The sheriff came striding in and stopped near them. His collar was soaked, his face red.

'Hyah, Banty,' greeted the deputy.

'Who the hell left that bottle on my desk?' he demanded.

'How was it?' asked Van Avery.

The sheriff glanced from Handsome to Van Avery.

'You go to hell, will you?' he snapped, and walked out.

'It was worth thirty dollars,' choked Van Avery. 'Let's have some more of this docile stuff.'

Hashknife did not put in an appearance until after Silver Steele had gone. Ken had heard about Hashknife's disappearance, and he was rather shocked to find him alive and well. But he was no more surprised than Hashknife was when they explained why Ken was out of jail.

Hashknife had not the slightest idea who had switched those guns, but he congratulated Ken.

'What good is it goin' to do you to hide out?' asked Ken.

'Nobody ever tries to kill a dead man.' Hashknife grinned.

'Well, do you have to stay here?'

'Ken!' said Gladys reprovingly.

177

'Oh, I didn't mean it the way it sounded, honey. I meant that—'

'I know what you meant,' said Hashknife condoningly.

'Hashknife has risked his life for us,' said Elene. 'He and Sleepy have been working here, and working hard, with no hope of being paid.'

'I appreciate that,' replied Ken. 'We never can do enough for them; but I'm naturally curious as to what Hashknife intends to do.'

'There's a lot more people who would wonder the same thing if they knew he was alive,' said Sleepy.

'Never mind that part of it,' interrupted Hashknife. 'I'm no bogey man, and I'm not so darned smart. Do any of you know if Mr. Corey done this year's assessment work on them claims he located out there along the north line fence?'

'He didn't,' replied Ken. 'I asked him about it, and he said there was no use because they're no good. He merely did it to stop Nelson.'

'Why did you want to know about them?' asked Elene.

'Oh, I was jist curious.'

The Coreys were a happy family at supper that night. Hashknife was served in the cellar, because he was afraid somebody might drop in and see him there.

He talked things over with Sleepy, and about nine o'clock he sneaked out to the stable, saddled his horse, and headed into the dark hills. No one, except Sleepy, knew he was going to Painted Wells; and Sleepy did not know exactly why Hashknife was going. Hashknife wasn't exactly sure himself, but he had an idea.

He tied his horse behind a shed at the rear of Nelson's store and assay office. He knew that Nelson slept in the rear of his store and that Dave Bush lived with a family on the outskirts of town. It was too early for Rick Nelson to be in bed; so Hashknife went quietly to the two back windows of the assay office.

One of them seemed to be nailed tightly, but the other slacked a little under pressure. Assuring himself that everything was all right, he lifted the warped window high enough to allow him to crawl in over the sill. He had been in the assay office once and was familiar with its arrangement.

There was a small stairway at the rear, which led down to a basement. Moving with the stealth of an Indian, Hashknife descended it. The air was redolent of acids, and he decided that Rick Nelson did most of his assaying there.

In the cellar he scratched a match and looked around. Here were the furnaces, test-tubes, acids—all the paraphernalia of a complete assay office. With the aid of scratched matches he searched carefully but swiftly.

Suddenly came a jarring sound. A test-tube tinkled. Hashknife blew out the match and stood in the inky blackness wondering what had caused that jar. His mind worked swiftly. Next door, with only a six-foot alley between them, was the Painted Wells Bank. His ears were intent for the slightest sound, but everything was quiet.

He went softly over to the bottom of the stairs, and he thought he heard a man running on the wooden sidewalk. He listened closely and suddenly ducked back away from the stairs. Someone was trying to unlock the back door of the assay office. He came in, and Hashknife heard him clashing the key against the lock, trying to secure the door behind him.

Hashknife could hear noises from the street now, as the man came down the stairs, passing within ten feet of him as he crossed the room. Then there came the creak of a cabinet door, and in a few moments the man, breathing heavily, passed Hashknife again and went up the stairs.

He apparently let himself out onto the street, because Hashknife heard the click of a lock as the man closed an upper door. Hashknife lighted a match and swiftly crossed the cellar to an old cabinet. On a shelf was a canvas grain-sack. It was not empty. Hashknife reached inside it and drew out a bundle of currency. Quickly he took it under his arm and went back to the stairs, hurrying up to the open window.

There was no doubt in his mind that the bank had been robbed and that this was the loot; but he had no idea of the identity of the man who had tried to cache it in the basement. Neither did he know that the sheriff and several men had already started a search. The jar of the explosion had given the robbers little time to clean up the vault and make a getaway.

Hashknife slid over the sill and hurried toward his horse. As he went around the corner of the old shed, he almost bumped into a man. It was a shock to both of them, but Hashknife recovered first. He crashed the man against the shed, knocking a gun from his hand, and in the dim starlight he recognized Van Avery.

The recognition was mutual.

'Don't make a yip, Blondy,' said Hashknife softly. 'Play the game, kid.'

Van Avery could only gurgle. Someone was yelling Van Avery's name from the alley. Hashknife sprang to his horse. Van Avery didn't answer. In fact, he didn't move until the thudding hoofs died away in the night. Men were running down the alley, and Handsome was the first to reach him.

Van Avery was down, gasping wheezingly for breath. They helped him to his feet, trying to find out what happened to him. It was several moments before he was able to gasp out his story. He had obeyed the sheriff's orders to circle that side of the street. Behind this shed, deep in the shadow, he had found a saddled horse. But before he had a chance to yell, a man seemed to come from nowhere, knocked the gun out of his hand, knocked all the air out of his lungs, and escaped on the horse.

Van Avery's description was very vague. He said the man was strong, very sudden and very rough. It was too dark to see his face. The horse was either a bay or a black, possibly a brown or a sorrel; it was too dark to say positively.

'You're a hell of a lot of help, all right,' mourned Handsome. 'The son of a gun prob'ly had all that money with him.'

'He didn't say,' panted Van Avery.

'Prob'ly didn't know who you was,' said Handsome dryly. 'These here Arizony bank robbers never git confidential with anybody they never been introduced to, you know.'

A check of the vault showed that the robbers got something like eleven thousand dollars for their night's work. The rear door had been cleverly jimmied and the locks snapped off clean. But they had made the mistake of using too much nitroglycerin, nearly wrecking the interior of the building.

Banty Brayton was too angry for words—so angry that Handsome refrained from making any smart remarks. Rick Nelson, Ed Ault, Van Avery, Mark Hawker, and several other men stood around the office and listened to a discourse in profanity. Banty singled out Van Avery.

'Why the hell didn't I send a man in your place?'

'I'll bite,' replied Van Avery innocently. 'Why didn't you?'

'Had him in your hands,' wailed the sheriff.

'I beg your pardon; I had him on my chest.'

'Yeah? Why didn't you shoot him?'

'Well'—Van Avery smiled weakly—'he knocked my gun out of my hand, and my finger wouldn't go off. I'm sorry.'

Handsome doubled over with mirth.

'His finger wouldn't go off. Betcha forty dollars he tried it.'

'What's to be done now, Banty?' asked Nelson.

'Done? What in hell can we do? Man got away, didn't he? What do you want to do—take up a collection for the bank?'

'I'll give a dollar,' offer Van Avery.

'Will you git out of here?' roared the exasperated sheriff. 'If you can't find your way out, I'll give you a map.'

'Aw, hell, he done all he could, Banty,' said Handsome.

'You stickin' up for this mockin'-bird?'

'I'm tryin' to figure out a way to keep you from makin' a damn fool out of yourself. You act like you'd lost the money.'

'I'm the sheriff of this county.'

'Oh, excuse me, I thought you was an auctioneer.'

'And you're fired, Handsome. No damn hired help can—'

'Wait a minute,' warned Handsome. 'I'm fired. Good; that's settled. The rest of your remarks won't do either of us any good.'

Handsome took off his badge of office and tossed it on the table.

'If applications are in order,' said Van Avery, 'I'd like to—'

'You'd what?' roared the sheriff.

'I'd just like to say that I'm not putting in any for the job.'

Van Avery walked out, making a dignified exit.

'If there's nothin' further we can do—' observed Nelson.

'Further?' groaned the sheriff. 'What have you done so far, Rick?'

'Well, we—we listened to you,' interjected Hawker, and walked to the door, followed by the others.

Handsome dug into the desk and began removing some of his personal property. The sheriff looked at him with pained eyes.

'You ain't really quittin', are you, Handsome?' he asked.

Handsome looked up quickly.

'You really fired me, didn't you, Banty?'

'Oh, that! You make me mad, sometimes. Why ain't you never serious?'

'Does bein' serious ever git you anythin',
Banty?'

The sheriff sighed deeply.

'It ain't yet. Mebbe it will sometime.'

'Git you a poke in the snoot, tha's all.'

'Uh-huh. I wish they hadn't got Hashknife.'

Handsome nodded as he pinned the shield on
his vest again.

'We'll ride around tomorrow,' said the sheriff
meekly. 'Got to act like we was doin' somethin',
I reckon.'

'Act smart,' agreed Handsome, 'even if we both
know that our combined brains wouldn't make a
subconscious mind for a chickadee.'

CHAPTER IX
SAFE-BUSTER

Van Avery did not sleep much that night. He wondered whether he had done the right thing. Why had Hashknife ordered him to play the game? The shock of seeing Hashknife alive and well had been enough to prevent Van Avery from doing very much. Had Hashknife robbed the bank? Van Avery had seen that bundle under his arm.

He tried to link Hashknife with the robbery at the mine, but was unable to do so. Was Hashknife one of the gang? Had he switched from working with the law? Van Avery couldn't quite figure out why Hashknife Hartley had made such a quick getaway, unless he had been one of the robbers— possibly the only one. And Hashknife had warned him to be quiet.

'Well, I played the game,' Van Avery told himself grimly. 'Right or wrong, I played his game. I'm either loyal or dumb.'

The next morning Van Avery rode out of town and headed for the ranch, while Banty and Handsome saddled their horses and made a pretense of searching for the robbers of the bank.

Hashknife had not told anyone what had happened in Painted Wells, but when Sleepy warned him that Van Avery had reached the ranch, Hashknife said to send Van Avery down to see him alone. Van Avery did not seem properly surprised when Sleepy told him that Hashknife was in the cellar and wanted to see him.

Van Avery shook hands with the women and went down the steps. He found Hashknife taking life easy on a cot. Sleepy closed the cellar door after Hashknife lighted the lamp.

'Was you surprised last night?' asked Hashknife.

'It was rather a shock,' admitted the young man. 'I thought I had met a ghost.'

Hashknife laughed softly.

'Thank you for playin' the game, Blondy.'

'I didn't understand, Hashknife; but I tried to— well, I didn't tell who you were.'

'That's playin' the game. See this?' Hashknife reached under the cot and drew out the canvas sack. 'There's about eleven thousand in that sack, Blondy.'

Van Avery looked at it uneasily. He could be accused as an accessory to this robbery. He blinked in the yellow light.

'How would you like to have half of it, Blondy?' asked Hashknife.

'Not me,' replied Van Avery quickly. 'I—I couldn't do that. Gee, I wish you hadn't asked me that, Hashknife. It's all right. I don't care what you do, but I couldn't do a thing like that. I like you and Sleepy.'

Hashknife smiled and began rolling a cigarette.

'Blondy,' he said, 'I believe you're an honest man.'

'Yes, I am,' Van Avery answered simply.

'Never stole anythin', eh?'

'Certainly not.'

'What about the time you opened the sheriff's safe and took out that gun?'

Van Avery's jaw sagged and his face flushed.

'Of course,' continued Hashknife, 'it wasn't exactly a theft, 'cause you left a better gun than you took away. Legally, you'd be in a hell of a mess if the prosecutin' attorney knew about it.'

Van Avery sat down on the end of the cot.

'Well,' he said huskily, 'you've got me there. What do you want?'

Hashknife looked at him severely for several moments; but slowly a smile wrinkled his lean face.

'I want to hug you, you damn maverick; and then I want you to tell me how you done it.'

'You mean—you're not going to tell on me?'

'I wouldn't even mention it in a prayer. Go ahead and tell me.'

Convinced that everything was all right, Van Avery told Hashknife how he swapped guns. He knew that both Handsome and the sheriff had a key to the safe, and that this gun was the main evidence against Ken.

'I didn't know how to get that key,' he told Hashknife. 'I never was a heavy drinker, and I had no hopes of getting Handsome drunk; but I made up my mind I had to do it. I was going to merely steal Ken's gun; but when I went behind the bar to serve the drinks, I saw that gun. I didn't know who owned it, but I took it anyway.

'I knew Handsome was pretty drunk, but I also realized that I was little better. When we went back to the office, Handsome sprawled on the cot and began snoring. That was my chance, and I made the most of it. I can hardly remember opening that safe and making the exchange, but I remember I had a hard time getting the key back in Handsome's pocket. I was sure they wouldn't miss the gun until the trial; so I hid it in my valise until I had a chance to throw it in the brush. Wasn't I sick! But it was worth being sick, wasn't it?'

'You bet it was,' replied Hashknife warmly. 'Now I've got a little confession to make to you, Blondy; I never stole that money from the bank.'

'You didn't?'

'I stole it from the man who stole it from the bank. In other words, I hijacked it.'

'Did you know the man?'

'No, I don't know who he is; but I think I'll

find out soon. The bank will git their money back, don't worry about that.'

Van Avery impulsively held out his hand.

'Hashknife, I want you to forgive me for what I thought.'

'You evened that up when you played the game with me. Suppose they had caught me with that money. Me supposed to be missing, and they get me with the goods. Can't you see what would happen to me, Blondy?'

Blondy nodded.

'I guess it would go hard with you, Hashknife.'

'Yeah, quick and hard.'

'Well, I'm glad I had a little sense—for once in my life.'

'Mebbe you've reformed,' Hashknife smiled. Then his face hardened, and his keen gray eyes studied the young man for several moments. 'Blondy,' he said, 'have you got nerve enough to do a dangerous piece of work?'

'How dangerous?' countered Van Avery.

'That's a problem. Listen to this.'

Hashknife lowered his voice and talked swiftly for five minutes.

'That doesn't sound dangerous,' said Van Avery. 'It really seems simple to me.'

'It might mean a bullet in the back, Blondy.'

Van Avery thought it over carefully before giving his decision.

'I don't understand just what it will mean, but

I'll do it. There's nothing illegal about it, so far as I can see.'

While they were talking, the sheriff and deputy, riding past, stopped at the ranch and told the Coreys about the robbery. Van Avery managed to sneak out of the cellar while the rest of them were in the patio, and he came out to meet the officers. The sheriff had probably forgiven Van Avery, because he did not mention the fact that Van Avery had failed to hold the fleeing robber. They were going back to town, so Van Avery rode back with them.

The robbery of the bank was another shock to Silver Steele. He was a heavy stockholder in the little organization, and it meant that the stockholders would be obliged to make up this loss. He was in the Yucca Saloon, standing at the bar with Ed Ault, when Handsome and Van Avery came in.

'Anythin' new, Handsome?' asked Silver.

'Nope,' replied Handsome wearily. 'I knew there wouldn't be, Silver. How could there be? I tell you, you've gotta nail 'em on the job, if you're ever goin' to get 'em.'

'Van Avery workin' with you?' asked Ault.

'He is not,' said Van Avery stiffly. 'Regardless of the fact that a number of misguided, would-be murderers around here thought I might be a detective, I'm not any such thing. I hope they are satisfied now.'

'You had me fooled.' Silver Steele laughed. 'I thought you was the man the Association sent in here to help me out.'

'I guess I'm lucky to be alive,' Van Avery smiled and motioned to the bartender to fill their glasses.

'How are things out at the Diamond C?' asked Ault.

'All right,' grunted Handsome, trickling a little water into his liquor. 'Sleepy is still out there, wanderin' around, wonderin' where his pardner went.'

'I'd like to know that myself,' said Steele.

'I guess they got him,' remarked Ault. 'Well, here's regards.'

They drank together and the glasses rattled back on the bar.

'Frazer was part conscious this mornin',' stated Steele. 'Said a few words and went under again. Doc Smedley says they've got hopes he'll eventually pull through. I hope he recognized the men who slugged him.'

'I'm jist scared he won't,' sighed Handsome. 'He was hit from behind, you know. We figure he was writin' a letter, askin' somebody for the name of a safe-buster.'

'Safe-buster?' asked Ault.

'The letter was smeared with ink,' explained Handsome. 'Couldn't see who he was writin' to. Hashknife figured that Frazer rec'nized somebody as bein' a expert safe-buster, and he wanted information about him and his name.'

'Did he mention any names in the letter?' asked Ault.

'I don't remember. Don't think he did, except the names of the lawyers who defended this feller, whoever he is.'

'I've sure had a run of hard luck,' remarked Steele.

'You had one break of good luck when they turned Ken loose,' reminded Ault.

'Lucky to get him loose, but it don't prove who killed Corey.'

'I wouldn't let that worry me.' Ault smiled. 'But I'll be damned if I wouldn't like to get my hands on the jigger who stole my gun and put it in the safe. I remember puttin' that gun under the bar where it would be handy for the bartender in case of trouble. I don't know how long it has been gone.'

'It looks to me as though Ken was very wise in not talking at the inquest and at the preliminary hearing,' said Van Avery. 'He refused to admit ownership of the gun. And the prosecutor failed to make a complete description of the gun.'

'He probably never expected the evidence to be stolen,' said Handsome. 'Anyway, it was weak evidence to hang a man on. I never did believe Ken killed Milt Corey.'

Steele turned to Ault.

'If you'll make out a bill for what Ken owes

you, Ed, I'll pay his debts and you can release Ken's property.'

'Oh, all right, Silver.'

'I think I'll take over the Diamond C,' said Van Avery casually.

'You'll what?' grunted Silver Steele.

'Pay off that bank mortgage,' replied Van Avery. 'It's worth the money.'

'Let me get this straight,' said Ault quickly. 'You mean you are goin' to pay off that ten thousand to the bank?'

'That's about the only way I could get it, is it not? I think the place is worth more money than that.'

'Listen to me,' said Ault. 'Perhaps you don't know I loaned Milt Corey ten thousand. When you add that to the mortgage money, you'd be losin' your shirt on the deal.'

'Would you mind letting me see that note?' asked Van Avery.

Ault lost no time in getting the note from his safe. It was merely a promissory note for ten thousand, due six months from date. Van Avery glanced at it and shoved it aside.

'That's merely a personal note,' he said. 'The signer is dead.'

'Is that so!' snapped Ault, his face getting red. 'It happens that the Diamond C is in Milt Corey's name, and I can collect from his estate. Just think that over a minute.'

'I'm afraid that is true, Van Avery,' said Steele.

Van Avery laughed softly.

'Wrong guess all the way around. What is to prevent me from paying off that mortgage? Nothing. That paper is killed. Then Mrs. Corey sells me the property, and I deed it back to her, in her name. When I buy it from her, I assume that note; but when I deed it back to her, I still assume that note. She gets the property free and clear of all encumbrances.'

Ault's jaw sagged foolishly, and he stared at Van Avery.

'You'd merely be assumin' a ten-thousand-dollar debt,' remarked Silver Steele.

'That is all very true. Ault could sue me and get judgment.'

'By Heaven, I'd take that money out of your hide!' snapped Ault.

Van Avery nodded thoughtfully.

'And that might be the only way you'd ever get it, Mr. Ault.'

'You figurin' on goin' into the cow business?' asked Handsome.

'No, I don't believe I will. But I am interested in mining. No, I don't know a thing about mines. One rock looks the same as another to me. But I've got a little money to spend, and I think I'll take over those claims that Milt Corey staked inside his north fence.'

Silver Steele laughed and motioned for the bartender to serve them.

'Those claims are no good,' said Steele. 'Save your money. Corey merely located them to block Rick Nelson because he disliked Rick. That whole rim down there wouldn't assay four bits in gold.'

'Well, I don't know about the values'— Van Avery laughed—'but it looks like a dandy place to dig.'

'When is all this diggin' goin' to start?' asked Ault coldly.

'Oh, in a few days. I'm not in any hurry. I may go down to Red Hill tomorrow, because I've got to go to Phoenix for a few days. This deal will require money, even if I don't do any mining. I'll bring an engineer back here to go over the property and suggest what I need.'

'You'll need payin' ore more than anythin' else.' Steele laughed.

Ault was worried. After Handsome and Van Avery left the saloon, he asked Steele if he thought Van Avery was sincere about paying off the Diamond C mortgage.

'I don't see why I should be the one to lose,' he said mournfully. 'I made that loan in good faith.'

'Maybe he was jokin',' encouraged Steele. 'He's a hard one to figure out. Your best bet would be to dig up the ten thousand and buy the mortgage from the bank. Van Avery would have to deal with you then.'

'That's an idea,' muttered Ault. 'Thanks, Silver.'

Fifteen minutes later, Ed Ault entered the bank. They were still checking up on the robbery loss; but Don Elkins, the cashier, came over to Ault.

'I want to talk a little business with you, Don,' said Ault. 'You've got a mortgage against the Diamond C, haven't you?'

'We foreclosed on it, and—'

'I know about that,' interrupted Ault. 'What I want to do is buy that mortgage.'

Elkins's eyes opened curiously.

'Somebody struck diamonds on that ranch?' he asked.

'Why?'

'Oh, I just wondered. Young Van Avery was in here a while ago and made a deal on that mortgage. He gave us a deposit of two thousand, and is to pay the rest within thirty days.'

'You mean I'm too late to buy it?'

'Yes, that's right, Ault.'

Ault took a deep breath and turned away.

'All right,' he said. 'I just wanted to help the Corey family out, that's all.'

'Sorry, but that's the way it stands now, Ault.'

Steele met Ault at the saloon door, but Ault did not mention that he was unable to deal with the bank.

Later in the afternoon Steve McCord and Ike Berry, of Porcupine, rode in to Painted Wells. Van Avery saw them tie their horses at the Yucca. McCord and Berry were the two cowboys he had had the trouble with in Porcupine, and he did not want to meet them. So he saddled his horse and headed for the ranch. Just before he reached the road to the Diamond C, he met a man driving a team and wagon.

The man was Brad Thatcher, from Porcupine. He looked curiously at Van Avery as they passed, but did not speak. Thatcher had not been at the X8X when Van Avery was there, but he knew him from descriptions. Van Avery did not know Thatcher, but he recognized the team as one which had been to Painted Wells from Porcupine before; so he decided that it was Steve McCord's freight wagon.

They gave Van Avery a warm welcome at the ranch and let him into the cellar to talk with Hashknife. He recounted, as nearly *verbatim* as possible, his conversation with Ault regarding the mortgage and the note. Hashknife grinned as Van Avery said that Ault swore he'd take the value of the note out of his hide.

'You kinda had Mr. Ault stuck, didn't you, Blondy? That's great. You done it better than I could.'

'I went further than that,' continued Blondy. 'I paid the bank a deposit of two thousand on that mortgage, and I've got thirty days to pay the rest. I just got to thinking that Ault might possibly do what I had said I was going to do. Anyway, I saw him go to the bank about fifteen minutes after I closed the deal.'

'I'd like to know who in hell circulated the report that you was dumb,' said Hashknife seriously. 'Who else did you see in town? This is Saturday, and there ought to be plenty folks.'

'Two men from Porcupine rode in just before I left, and I met the freight outfit from Porcupine just before I turned in here.'

'Yeah? Well, that's fine. Anythin' new on the robbery?'

'Not a thing. Did you know Silver Steele was a heavy stockholder in the bank? He is. And I heard him ask Ault to make out his bill against Ken, and he'd pay it in full. That was nice of him.'

'Steele is a white man, Blondy. What about Frazer?'

'He was almost conscious once today. I hope he gets well.'

'So do I. You go on upstairs and visit the folks, 'cause I want to do a little private thinkin'.'

Mrs. Corey and Elene had decided that they wanted to go to town after supper, and Sleepy was elected to drive the team. Ken and his wife were going to stay at the ranch. They asked Van Avery to stay and keep them company. The arrangement

199

was satisfactory, except that Van Avery wished it were Elene instead of Ken's wife.

It was almost dark when they were ready to leave. Sleepy went down in the cellar to have a talk with Hashknife. Fifteen minutes after they had gone, Hashknife came out of the cellar.

'I'm goin' to take a ride,' he said. 'If I'm not back until late, don't worry about me. You stay here all night, Blondy. I don't believe Painted Wells would be a safe place for you now. *Adios.*'

CHAPTER X
KIDNAPED

The lighted windows of the town partly illuminated the main street of Painted Wells as Sleepy and the two women drove in. Two riders, heading south, passed them, and Sleepy recognized Steve McCord and Ike Berry, of Porcupine.

Sleepy tied the team in front of the general store where the women wanted to do most of their shopping; they told him it would be an hour or more before they would be ready to return. They had little money for shopping, but the proprietor graciously informed them that their credit was still good. They did not know Silver Steele had told the merchant what Van Avery intended doing. The Diamond C had always been a good account.

Sleepy found Handsome in the street. His rubicund nose was just a little redder than usual and he was grinning. It was obvious that he had looked upon the wine when it was red and that he was seeking congenial company.

But Sleepy was not in a drinking mood. He had to look after the two women. Handsome appreciated that fact thoroughly.

'Where's Blondy?' he asked. 'Zassa feller I

want. Great feller. Got great capashity. Run out on me today. This's worsh Shaterday night I ever sheen. Can' find par'ner. Steve McCord and Ike Berry pulled out on me. You shore you don't wanna drink, Sleepy?'

'Nope. Like I told you, I've got to take care of m' women. And, besides, I ain't thirsty, Handsome.'

''S awful way for to be—not thirshty. Well, s'long. Temp'rance. See you at the rally in the church.'

Handsome went bowlegging his way back to the Yucca. Sleepy grinned after the little deputy, and went down the street, merely killing time. He bought some tobacco and wandered around to the hardware store.

Dave Bush had several customers. Sleepy hoisted himself up on a counter and rolled a smoke, watching Bush measure out a rope for a cowboy. Bush seemed nervous, and was obliged to measure the rope three times to be sure of the right length.

Next he weighed a few pounds of tenpenny nails, dumped them into a paper bag which split open, and the nails went all over the floor. Instead of weighing out another lot, he got down on his hands and knees and picked up the nails, perspiration glistening on his nose.

Sleepy studied Bush thoughtfully. Sleepy was not ordinarily observant, but Bush's nervousness was very plain. Finally he cleared out the customers and went to the rear of the room, mopping his face with a handkerchief.

Another customer came in, carrying a five-gallon kerosene can. Sleepy saw that it was the swamper from the Yucca.

Bush came forward slowly. The man gave Bush the can.

'I don't see why you always wait until dark,' complained Bush pettishly. 'When the sun goes down, you realize the need of oil.'

The swamper grinned at Sleepy as Bush went out through the back door, heading for the shed where he stored his kerosene.

'Kinda touchy t'night, ain't he?' queried the swamper.

'Acts thataway,' Sleepy smiled.

Bush did not shut the back door.

As Sleepy's eyes shifted, he saw the flash of a gun and heard the sharp bark of its report. Two more flashes came almost together and a double report followed.

The swamper grunted a curse. Silver Steele and Rick Nelson were coming through the front doorway, and they too heard the reports. Sleepy ran from the store, gun in hand, with Steele and Nelson behind him. The swamper, unarmed, followed more cautiously.

They found Dave Bush sprawled in front of the little shed. He was dead. They sent for

Dr. Smedley, but there was nothing he could do except in his capacity as coroner. A crowd collected around the corpse, and everyone demanded an answer to the question—

'Who killed him?'

No one knew the answer. So far as they knew, Bush had no enemies.

'At least two men did the shooting,' declared the doctor. 'One shot was in his back, two in the front.'

Rick Nelson closed the hardware store. Sleepy went up to the general store and found that Elene and her mother had already heard of the murder. They were so excited and shocked that they wanted to go home at once. They had known Dave Bush.

'What in the world are we coming to?' asked Mrs. Corey nervously. 'Poor Dave Bush, who never harmed anyone.'

Sleepy wondered why Dave Bush had been so nervous. Did he know someone was after him?

'What are you thinking about, Sleepy?' asked Elene.

'Oh,' he answered lightly, 'I look thataway when I git awful dumb. Ready to go home?'

Handsome, sobered by the tragedy, came up to Sleepy while he was taking the ropes off the team.

'Can you imagine a thing like that?' asked Handsome. 'And you was in the store and seen the flashes, eh? Poor old Dave. By golly, that's a tough thing to have happen! You didn't see Brad Thatcher, didja?'

'No,' replied Sleepy, coiling up the two ropes. 'He wasn't lookin' for me, was he?'

'He wasn't lookin' for nothin', except his team and wagon.'

'Team and wagon? He didn't lose 'em, did he?'

'Says he did. Had his stuff all loaded to take back to Porcupine, and now he can't find his outfit.'

'Somebody playin' a joke on him?'

'I think he got drunk and forgot where he tied the team, if you ask me,' Handsome laughed. 'Well, I've got to go down to the office and listen to Banty cry for a while, I suppose.'

'Why would anybody steal a team and wagon?' wondered Elene.

Sleepy laughed and climbed into the seat.

'I dunno,' he replied. 'I've come to the conclusion that most anythin' can happen around here. This doggone country is hoodooed, I tell you.'

'I'll be glad when we get home,' declared Elene. 'I don't know why, but I feel that everything isn't all right.'

'Oh, everything is all right there,' said Sleepy reassuringly.

They drove to the fork of the road and turned in toward the ranch.

'There isn't a light in the house,' declared Elene nervously.

'Curtains down,' said Sleepy.

'No lights anywhere,' said Elene. 'Ken would think to light a lantern at the main gate.'

'Mebbe not. You'll find everythin' all right. You're jist nervous over what happened in town.'

'It's enough to make a body nervous,' said Mrs. Corey. 'With all these murders.'

Sleepy swung the team in close to the corral and quickly tied one of the horses to the fence. Someone should hear them drive in and show a light. Elene was hurrying toward the house when Sleepy caught up with her.

'Me first,' he said softly. 'I—I think everythin' is all right.'

They went in through the patio gate. Everything was in darkness. Sleepy swore inwardly as he went up to the back door, which was open. In the darkness he heard a fumbling sort of noise. Whipping out his gun, he braced his shoulder against the side of the doorway.

'What's wrong in there?' he asked.

'Can'tcha help me a little?' groaned a voice. 'I can't find the water.'

Sleepy jerked out a match and struck it against the wall. There was Ken Steele on the floor, trying to sit up, with blood running down his cheeks.

'My God!' gasped Elene. 'Ken, what happened? Ken, don't you hear me?'

'Take it easy,' advised Sleepy. 'Wait'll I get the lamp.'

'On the table,' panted Mrs. Corey. 'Hurry, Sleepy.'

When the lamp was lighted, Sleepy gave Ken a drink. Ken was weak, but fully conscious. Sleepy noticed a red weal across the back of Ken's right hand; he had apparently been struck a savage blow over the head.

Sleepy promptly searched the house. There was no one else present. Hashknife had told Sleepy he might go out—but where were Gladys and Van Avery? Sleepy went back to Ken, who was trying to remember what had happened.

'I'm not much hurt,' he declared. 'Never mind me, Ma. My head feels fine now. Wasn't Sleepy with you? Oh, there you are, Sleepy.'

Sleepy appreciated the fact that Ken was just a bit light-headed.

'But where are the others, Ken?' asked Mrs. Corey. 'Mr. Van Avery and Gladys.'

'I dunno. Ain't they here? Why, I—I—my God, what happened to them? Those three men, all masked with black cloths. They sneaked in on us. Van Avery was tryin' to play on the guitar, and Glad was singin'. They warned us not to move, but I was afraid of what they might do; so I took a long chance.'

Ken stopped and looked at his swollen right hand.

'One of them shot my gun out of my hand,' he

said slowly. 'I don't remember what happened then.'

'Somebody socked you over the head with a gun-barrel, it looks to me,' said Sleepy.

Ken nodded painfully.

'I suppose that's what happened; but what happened to Glad and Blondy?'

Mrs. Corey and Elene looked at each other pitifully.

'Hashknife went out, Ken?' asked Sleepy.

'He went out soon after you folks left. Can I have another drink of water? I've got to get on my feet and help you find 'em.'

Sleepy gave him another drink.

'You lay down,' he said huskily. 'You ain't in no shape to ride anywhere. Lord, I wish Hashknife would show up. He'd know somethin' to do, mebbe. No use goin' for the sheriff. He'd be as good as a pair of loose crutches lookin' for a cripple. If I only—'

There came the scuffling of boot-soles on the porch, and Hashknife came in. He needed only a glance to know that something had gone wrong; and in a few short sentences Sleepy told him as much as any of them knew. Hashknife's lean face was gray in the lamplight. Sleepy told him about the murder of Dave Bush; told him in brief detail all the things that led up to the shooting, as far as he could remember.

Mrs. Corey sat stunned and helpless while

Elene tried to assure her that everything would be all right.

'Saddle your bronc, Sleepy,' said Hashknife. 'We're takin' a long ride tonight. Elene, you and your mother are safe here. Make the best of it. Ken, you go to bed, and tomorrow we'll turn the doctor loose on your topknot.'

'I'm goin' with you,' declared Ken.

'Not in the shape you're in, kid.'

'Have you any idea, Hashknife'—asked Elene shakily—'any idea what happened or why they took Gladys?'

'Not now, I ain't. But they won't hurt her. Somethin' went wrong, and they had to take her. You quit worryin'. I've just about built a loop big enough to hang the whole bunch of 'em.'

Sleepy came running up the steps to the doorway.

'All set!' he panted. 'Don't worry, folks. I'm jist scared to death that everythin' is goin' to be all right.'

Two minutes later the two cowboys were galloping down the dusty road toward Red Hill, not thinking of ambush this time. Both horses were in good shape; and for once in their lives these two cowboys were not sparing their horses.

Fifteen miles to Red Hill. Except for a lighted saloon, Red Hill was dark and seemingly deserted. But they did not stop; merely rode slowly through the town, found the road to

Porcupine, and spurred their horses to a gallop. This road was strange to them, but they knew it followed the railroad to Porcupine.

A passenger train rocketed past them, the engineer whistling for Porcupine. Their horses were exhausted as they came to Porcupine—a huddle of three adobe buildings beside the railroad tracks. There was one light in the little saloon; and a bareheaded man, presumably the bartender, was standing in the doorway as they rode up with their horses breathing loudly.

'Could you tell me how to find the X8X outfit?' asked Hashknife.

'Shore could,' replied the man. 'Take that road runnin' to the right out there a piece, and it'll take you right to the ranch. It ain't more'n a mile or so.'

Hashknife thanked him, and they rode on. In a few minutes they found the place—a dark group of old buildings. No lights were visible.

'Do you think we'll find 'em here?' asked Sleepy.

'If we don't, it eliminates one possible place,' muttered Hashknife as they dismounted in the darkness beside the old stable. 'Shore don't look good to me—everythin' dark thisaway. But we're here and we'll see what we can see. One cinch, they won't expect us tonight.'

They left their horses and crept in near the main ranch-house. There was a chance that the windows had been covered to cut off the light, but Hashknife found a window in the main room where he could see that this was not the case. It was a keen disappointment to Hashknife.

Apparently the place was empty. Hashknife and Sleepy crouched against the house, wondering what move to make next, when they heard a horse galloping. It came straight to the house, stopping near the corner and not over a dozen feet away. They saw the rider dismount. The horse was blowing heavily, from a long, hard run. They heard the man crash open the front door, and from somewhere in the house they heard someone yell a question.

Hashknife and Sleepy crept past the horse and under the sagging railing of the porch. The door was still open. A lamp was being lighted, and two men were talking. Hashknife got to his feet, flat against the wall, where he could peer around the room.

Standing with his back to the doorway was Brad Thatcher, while on the other side of a rough table was a bearded man, dressed only in an ill-fitting suit of red underwear. He had apparently been in bed and asleep when Thatcher arrived.

'No, Jim, I'm pullin' out,' Thatcher was saying. 'I'm goin' to be a hell of a long ways from Painted Wells by daylight.'

'Won't the rest of the boys—' began the bearded man.

'To hell with everybody,' said Thatcher huskily. 'They won't be back tonight. Somebody stole the team and wagon. Bush is dead. I lifted me a bronc from a hitch-rack and pulled out. And I found the team and wagon this side of the Diamond C turn-off. Somebody's wise, I tell you; the box was gone!'

'Them shells?' asked the bearded one thinly.

'Gone, I tell you!'

'Yeah?' The bearded one shivered slightly. 'Well, I told you, Brad. Ain't I argued with the bunch to be good? Didn't they laugh at me for tryin' to tell 'em that crooked work allus bends back on you? I'm only a damn old cook, but I spent fourteen years in Deer Lodge, Montana; and you can't tell me nothin' about crime bein' a payin' proposition.'

'Don't preach! You're safe, 'cause you never had no hand in it. Mebbe they'll hang you on general principles—I dunno. But I know damn well they won't git me. To hell with the money— I'm savin' my neck.'

'Uh-huh. You shore must 'a' made a fast trip down here.'

'Cut across the hills from Painted Wells and hit the road between here and Red Hill.'

'What about the rest of the bunch, Brad? Do they know what happened? You ain't leavin' 'em dry-gulched, are you?'

'I'm through, I tell you,' snarled Thatcher. 'Let

'em save their own skins. I've got enough to keep me a long time down in Mexico.'

'But who got wise?' asked the cook. 'Banty Brayton ain't got brains enough to—'

'What do I care who got wise? I'm—'

The floor creaked as Hashknife stepped in through the doorway. Thatcher whirled around. His eyes opened wide and he sagged back against the table. Hashknife stood hunched forward, his long hands hanging at his sides.

Thatcher's left hand came up, clawlike, and trembled over his sagging mouth. He was looking at the ghost of a dead man. Hashknife's lips moved slowly with his voice pitched in a low monotone—

'You're goin' on a long trip, Thatcher—but not to Mexico.'

'Damn you to hell!' screamed Thatcher, as he reached for his gun.

At the same moment Sleepy fired from the doorway, and Thatcher fell against the table, then collapsed in a heap. Hashknife was on him like a tiger and tore the gun out of his hand. The old cook did not move, merely shifted his eyes from one to the other.

Hashknife lifted the lamp off the table and knelt down beside Thatcher, who was looking up at him, a glare in his eyes.

'Come through clean,' said Hashknife. 'Where did they take that girl tonight?'

Thatcher blinked painfully.

'What girl?' he asked, and Hashknife realized Thatcher was innocent of that charge.

'They kidnaped Ken Steele's wife tonight,' said Hashknife.

'I—I didn't know it,' gasped Thatcher. 'Turn that lamp up a little. I—I can't see you.'

'He won't go to Mexico,' said the cook dully.

Hashknife got to his feet and looked at the cook.

'I heard what Thatcher and you talked about,' said Hashknife. 'It means that I'm givin' you a chance to pull out. Don't be here when they come to bury Thatcher.'

'You are givin' me a chance to get away?' asked the old man.

'Unless you want to stay and testify against 'em.'

The old cook shook his head.

'Not agin men I've cooked for for five years.'

'Then don't be here, pardner. Are there any fresh horses on the place?'

'Six of 'em in the stable. We allus keeps a string handy. Jist who in hell are you, anyway?'

'My name's Hartley.'

'Hashknife Hartley? The hell it is! Well'— eyeing Hashknife in amazement—'I don't blame Brad for screamin'. You're the first ghost I ever seen, close to.'

Hashknife reached out and picked up a letter from the table.

'When didja git this?' asked Hashknife.

'This mornin'. I went as far as Red Hill with the boys.'

It was addressed to Steve McCord, and the letterhead was that of the San Francisco Mint. Hashknife tore it open and drew out a statement, showing that the mint had credited the Hellbender Mining Company with eight thousand dollars' worth of gold.

Hashknife shoved the letter in his pocket and turned to the cook.

'We're borrowin' a couple fresh horses, pardner. I suppose it's all right with you.'

'Ort to be. I'm borrowin' one m'self.'

It was a long, weary night for the Corey family. None of them went to bed. Ken suffered from his scalp injuries, the ache almost blinding him at times. They were all trying to be patient, to do as Hashknife had asked them to do; but daylight was more than welcome.

Breakfast meant nothing to them. Elene harnessed the team, and the three of them headed for Painted Wells. Ken needed the services of a doctor.

'If Glad is only safe,' he said. 'That's all that matters to me.'

Less than a mile from Painted Wells they overtook the sheriff and deputy. Handsome was driving the X8X freight team, while Banty led

Handsome's horse. They had found the abandoned outfit and were bringing it back to town.

The sheriff rode in close to the buckboard, while Elene told him what had happened at the Diamond C ranch. Banty just looked at her with a dumb, wondering expression in his eyes. This was the straw that broke the camel's back. Without a word he galloped straight for town.

It was Sunday morning and there were many people in town, some of whom had been there all night. The sheriff went straight to the Yucca Saloon, where he faced those present and told them that it was time for every man in the county to help find Gladys Steele. In a few words he told them what had happened at the Corey ranch.

'We've got to smash that gang,' he declared hotly. 'It's plenty bad enough to murder men, but when they start kidnapin' our women, it's time to put an end to things.'

'All right,' said Ault briskly. 'What's the first move?'

The sheriff leaned against the bar, shaking his head.

'God only knows,' he said huskily. 'I'm jist the sheriff. Some of you think I ort to know what to do, but I don't. I ain't got no more idea than any of you have. They strike in the dark, and they don't leave no clues. Why in hell would they take a girl? Mebbe they think Van Avery is a detective. The damn fools ort to know better. He's no

216

detective. Why did they try to kill Judge Frazer? Why did they kill Dave Bush? What assurance have we that one of us won't be the next one to git it? Damn you, do a little thinkin', can'tcha?'

Silver Steele was there. Some of the men looked to him, but the big miner had no suggestions.

'Do you think I'd be standin' here listenin' if I knew anythin'?' he asked them. 'That girl is my son's wife. I believe that same gang murdered Milt Corey and tried to throw the blame on Ken. Last night they knocked him out and stole his wife. I agree with Banty that it's time to smash that gang—but how?

'There was one man—his name was Hartley— and I think he knew somethin'. But they got him. The prospector you knew as Jack Cherry, who was found dead in Rick Nelson's prospect hole, was murdered. His name was Payzant, and he was a detective hired by me. Mebbe Dave Bush knew somethin'. The same gang murdered Ryan and smashed my safe. They robbed the bank. It's time we put a stop to it. None of us are safe until that murderin' gang is wiped out.'

'Well, let's do somethin',' growled Steve McCord.

'You suggest somethin',' said Ault.

'I wish I could, Ed; but this is beyond me. I'll foller anybody who wants to lead.'

Someone mentioned that Handsome was

bringing in the missing freight team, and the crowd broke up to go over across the street. The load was covered with a tarpaulin. Steve McCord removed it to check the load. Rick Nelson was on the sidewalk, watching Steve.

'Is everythin' all right, Steve?' he asked.

The boss of the X8X looked it over, and his eyes narrowed thoughtfully. It wasn't all there and he knew it; but he nodded and said—

'All right, I guess.'

'What in hell was their idea of stealin' your wagon?' queried Handsome.

'You ask 'em,' retorted Steve evenly.

'I hope to.'

Steve looked at him closely.

'Yeah? Mind tellin' what makes you think so, Handsome?'

'I said I hoped to.'

'Oh!'

The sheriff drew Silver Steele aside.

'Was it true that somebody stole your horse and saddle last night?' he asked.

'They're gone,' said Steele. 'Mebbe broke loose, but I don't believe it, Banty.'

The sheriff nodded solemnly.

'I've been wonderin', Silver. Brad Thatcher drove that freight team in last night. Somebody stole his team and wagon. Brad Thatcher didn't stay here last night, and I can't find out how he got away. Never hired no horse.'

218

'Mebbe Steve would know; let's ask him.'

But Steve McCord didn't know. As he explained it:

'Me and Ike Berry wasn't goin' to wait for Brad, 'cause he'd take quite a while on the road with that heavy wagon. We had an eye on a poker game in Red Hill, and would meet Brad there. Well, we went down to Red Hill, and the poker game wasn't so good; but we stayed pretty late. In fact, it was long enough for Brad to have easy made the trip.

'Then we was afraid mebbe he broke down; so we started back to find him, which we didn't. We came all the way back here, and they said the team and wagon had been stolen. That looked pretty damn funny to us. We don't know where Brad went. He wasn't here.'

'Why do you suppose they stole the wagon?' asked the sheriff.

Steve laughed shortly.

'I pass, Banty. It's funny we didn't see that outfit beside the road, like Handsome said you found it.'

'Not so queer,' replied the sheriff. 'Whoever stole it drove off the road down there. The tracks are plenty plain. Then they drove back beside the road. You prob'ly passed while it was still off the road.'

It was a plausible explanation.

'We was wonderin' about Brad, 'cause Silver

had a horse and saddle stolen from the Yucca hitch-rack last night,' said Banty.

Steve looked curiously at Banty.

'Hell, you don't think Brad would steal a horse, do you?'

'I ain't accusin' nobody—yet. Brad never borrowed nor rented a horse last night.'

Steve laughed.

'I dunno. Things happen so fast around here that we can't even make a guess at any of them.'

The sheriff and Silver Steele went down to Doc Smedley's home, where they found the Corey family waiting for Ken to get patched up. They questioned Ken, trying to get some sort of description of the masked men; but Ken was unable to describe them.

'Where's Sleepy Stevens?' asked the sheriff.

'He went hunting for Glad and Van Avery,' said Elene truthfully. 'He rode away as soon as we got back home and found out what had happened out there.'

'Which way did he go?'

'None of us knew, and he didn't say where he was going.'

Steele and the sheriff went back to the street, where they met Steve McCord. He drew them aside and spoke confidentially.

'I've been wonderin' about that horse. I'd hate to think Brad would take a horse that didn't belong to him. In fact, I don't believe he did. But

I've sent Ike Berry down to the ranch to find out.'

'That's a mighty long ride to find out somethin',' said Silver.

'I want to know,' declared Steve. 'I won't harbor no horsethief, I'll tell you that. If we find out he did steal it, I'll make it right with you, Silver.'

'Oh, that's all right, Steve. I hate to put you to all that trouble.'

'Say! Trouble? I play square and I demand the same thing of my men.'

'Well, I hope I'm wrong,' Steele smiled.

CHAPTER XI
RIFLED GOLD

Shortly after the Corey family left the ranch, Hashknife and Sleepy, hungry and weary from their fifty-mile ride, came back. With the team and buckboard missing, they knew the family had gone to town. Hashknife cooked some breakfast, which bucked up their spirits a little.

They wound up the battered old alarm-clock, gave themselves a two-hour limit for sleep, and stretched out on the cot in the cellar. Sleepy could have sworn that he had only closed his eyes when the alarm went off. But he doused his head in a bucket of cold water and was soon wide awake again. He threw his saddle on one of the ranch horses and rode away, envying Hashknife, who stayed in the cellar.

He tied his horse behind the sheriff's office and was sauntering along the street before anyone noticed him; and it was not long until he was the center of attraction. But Sleepy was in a particularly uninspired mood. He didn't know a thing.

The sheriff, Silver Steele, and Steve McCord took him aside and plied him with questions, not one of which he could answer.

He told them how they had found things at the Diamond C.

'It didn't happen so awful long before we got there,' he said. 'So I jist piled onto a horse and went circlin' the country. I've been poundin' leather all night.'

'Why didn't you come right in and tell me?' asked the sheriff.

'What the hell could you have done?' retorted Sleepy. 'My only chance was to ride fast and pray for a little luck—which I didn't have. What was that report about somebody stealin' the X8X wagon?'

'We got it back,' growled Steve McCord. 'Some damn joker thought he'd have some fun.'

'You was here when Bush was shot, wasn't you?' asked the sheriff.

'I was in Nelson's store and saw the flashes of the guns.'

'That's right.'

'Where's the Corey family?'

'Down at Doc Smedley's place, I reckon.'

Sleepy went down there and found Ken asleep, his head and hand bandaged. Sleepy called Elene outside and told her that Hashknife said they had all better stay in town until he showed up. Elene was anxious for news, but Sleepy could tell her nothing.

'It was a terrible night, Sleepy,' she said. 'We never went to bed. I've been trying to get Mother to lie down awhile, but she's too worried. Oh, if we only had some idea where they took Glad.'

'I don't know a danged thing,' said Sleepy wearily. 'What Hashknife knows he keeps to himself. And he knows somethin'. Last night he was singin' on the way back.'

'Singing, Sleepy?'

'Well,' dryly, 'his kinda singin'.'

'I didn't mean that. But why should he sing?'

'That's his way, Elene. He allus sings when he sees his way clear to start for the tall hills agin.'

'I don't understand what you mean, Sleepy.'

He smiled at her and shook his head.

'We're a queer pair—me and Hashknife. But don'tcha worry. I'm just scared to death that everythin' is goin' to be all right.'

Silver Steele went out to his ranch and brought in all his cowboys. He offered them to the sheriff, who said he wouldn't know what to do with them.

'Well, they're here if you need 'em, Banty,' said Steele.

Sleepy listened to all the talk about forming a vigilante organization, and it rather amused him. There were plenty of armed men, plenty of ropes—and no one to hang. The sheriff was soured on everything. He looked upon the world with a jaundiced eye.

In fact, the whole place seemed at a standstill, waiting. But for what? The man-power of the

Painted Wells country was assembled, but no one knew of a wheel to turn.

'Jist like a lot of buzzards settin' around waitin' for somethin' to die,' declared Handsome.

'Yeah,' drawled Sleepy, 'and you'd be surprised if they got a good feed, wouldn't you?'

'I shore would, pardner. Another thing, I ain't goin' to stay here much longer. Reckon I'll trade my hundred and fifty a month for a forty-dollar job over in the Patagonia country. I crave to wake up in the mornin' and rassle with a cold-jawed bronc, instead of wakin' up every mornin' and tryin' to find out who killed somebody last night. I'm gittin' so skittish that I look under m' bunk every night; and if there ain't a killer cached under there, I crawl under and sleep there m'self.'

'I'm figurin' on goin' away pretty soon,' replied Sleepy. 'This country don't appeal to me none.'

'Which way you goin'?'

Sleepy's blue eyes smiled, but his mouth twisted grimly.

'You never know your luck,' he said soberly. 'Every mornin', when you start out, the cards are either stacked for you or against you. You never git a chance to cut or deal. You play blind, and the Big Dealer either gives you your share of the pot or He takes your last white chip. Then you drop out of the game for good. There's no chance to set in again.'

'That's a funny idea,' grunted Handsome.

'Mebbe it's right. You know, sometimes I wonder what in hell we're doin' around here, Sleepy. What's the use of what we're doin'? There's a lotta dead men, who done jist what we're doin', and what did they git out of it.'

'You keep on wonderin' about things like that, and some day I'll come and see how you're gettin' along in the loco lodge.'

'I suppose tha's right. Well, I ain't goin' to worry.'

Sleepy found a group of men at the Yucca bar, talking about Hashknife. Silver Steele, Rick Nelson, and Ed Ault were there. Sleepy joined them and listened to their conversation. Steele was of the opinion that Hashknife had known too much about the bad bunch; and it seemed to Sleepy that they had an idea Hashknife had told him things.

'He never told anybody what he knew,' said Sleepy. 'There never was a better man than my old pardner; and if he could come back right now, I'd bet ten dollars against a dime that he could tell you who done all this devilment.'

'That's what I think,' declared Steele.

'But they got him cold,' sighed Sleepy. 'If they hadn't, he'd have been back long before this.'

'I guess that's right,' nodded Nelson. 'This gang must be pretty smart.'

'How do you mean?' asked Sleepy.

'To spot Hartley as a detective.'

'Who said he was a detective?'

'Well, wasn't he?' asked Ault quickly.

'Mebbe that's my fault,' said Steele. 'You see, I asked the Association to send me the best man they could find. The wire I got made me feel that the man had been sent. I guess mebbe Van Avery fooled the bad bunch as much as he did me, 'cause they shore tried to kill him off. But he wasn't the detective at all.'

'So you decided that Hashknife was, eh?' grunted Sleepy. 'Oh, it don't matter now. They got him cold, detective or no detective.'

'Let's have another drink,' invited Ault.

About four o'clock Sleepy strolled into the empty sheriff's office, went out the back way, mounted his horse, and rode back to the ranch. He knew he had not been followed, so he saddled Hashknife's horse and tied both animals in a little canyon near the ranch-house.

Hashknife was anxious for news, and Sleepy told him everything that had been said during the day. He was particularly interested in what had been said about the stolen freight team, but Sleepy only knew that McCord had said that nothing was missing from the load.

Sleepy cooked some supper for them both; and as soon as it was dark they sneaked out to their horses. Sleepy had no idea where Hashknife would lead him. But that did not worry Sleepy.

He had never seen Hashknife more serious in his life; but the tall, drawn-faced cowboy was singing softly and mournfully:

And the cowboy riz up sadly
And mounted his cayuse,
Sayin', 'The time has come when longhorns
And cowboys ain't no use.'

And while gazin' sadly backward
Upon the dead bovine
His bronc stepped in a doghole
And fell and broke his spine.

'Singin' time agin, eh?' asked Sleepy.

'She's been a long time tunin' up,' replied Hashknife.

Hashknife led the way around to the east of Painted Wells. From where they skirted the open hills they could see the lights of the town. Their circle brought them toward the road to the Comanche Chief, but Hashknife decided to swing farther to the right again.

They rode steadily over this unfamiliar country, until to the west of them loomed the bulk of the Comanche Chief stamp mill and other buildings. They drew rein on the point of a hill and gave the horses a breathing spell. Down the valley below them winked the lights of Painted Wells.

There was one small light visible at the mine,

228

presumably in the office or in the assay room. They had rested their horses for about five minutes when the light suddenly disappeared. It came again for possibly ten seconds and then disappeared.

Hashknife grunted softly.

'Looked like a signal of some kind, Sleepy. That's why I didn't want to use the road. There's prob'ly a guard down there at the top of that long, steep pull, and he can git back there and notify 'em if anybody is comin'. C'mon.'

'Was you expectin' that signal?' asked Sleepy.

'No reason to expect it, and I don't even know what it might mean. But it's a cinch they ain't sendin' no warnin' about us.'

'I shore hope they ain't,' sighed Sleepy. 'I've seen better places to be buried in than Painted Wells.'

They rode within a hundred yards of the mine office, where they dismounted. It did not require much time to discover that the light was in the assay office, a tiny bit of it showing beneath the door.

They walked up close to the door, where they could hear the hum of muffled conversation. The doorknob creaked and the door was opened an inch or so. Someone was evidently coming out, but had stopped to say something to those in the room.

'—can't figure that stuff by the ton,' he said.

'Looks to me a lot richer than any we've got before. There ain't much of—'

His explanation was broken when Hashknife flung his weight against the door, fairly knocking the man back into the center of the room, where there were two men on their hands and knees beside a tarpaulin spread on the floor, on which were piled several pounds of ore.

The entrance of Hashknife and Sleepy was so sudden that the men merely gaped at them. Ortelle, the assayer, was on the floor, staring now at Hashknife through his thick glasses. He was looking at a ghost, and the sight did not please him. One of the men swore bitterly, but the gaze of the little assayer never wavered from Hashknife.

Sleepy looked them over calmly, his gun in his hand.

'That looks like high-grade stuff to me,' observed Hashknife dryly.

Ortelle licked his dry lips and tried to swallow. He shook his head and his glasses fell off.

'What's the idea?' croaked one of the other men.

'I'd hate to be as ignorant as you are,' Hashknife smiled. 'Go out and git our ropes, Sleepy. Mebbe you better look 'em over for guns.'

One man had a bulldog .44 in his hip pocket, but the rest were unarmed. Sleepy brought the ropes, and they proceeded to show those ore-thieves how a cowboy could hogtie a human. Ortelle didn't say a word. The appearance of Hashknife had numbed him.

'Goin' to leave 'em here or take 'em along?' asked Sleepy.

'That depends on Mr. Ortelle.'

'Me?' whispered Ortelle. It was his first vocal effort.

'Yeah, you, feller.' Hashknife hunched down in front of him.

'Where is Van Avery and Ken Steele's wife?'

Ortelle blinked foolishly at Hashknife, who looked sharply at the other prisoners. Hashknife knew in a moment that none of these men knew anything about it.

'I don't know,' whispered Ortelle. 'I don't even know what you are talking about.'

Hashknife took a deep breath and looked at Sleepy.

'Lord, that's good news!' he said thankfully. Turning back to the prisoners, he said—

'I'm leavin' you fellers here for a while.'

'Thank you,' said one of the men.

Hashknife smiled as he added:

'As soon as you show me the signal that brings your guard back here. You see, I can't have him turnin' you loose.'

The man swore caustically, but refused to talk further.

'What's the use?' choked out Ortelle. 'They'd

231

get him anyway. Lift up that window shade and leave it up.'

Sleepy flipped it up. Five minutes later the guard came whistling up the road and stepped in past Hashknife and Sleepy, who were at the door to greet him. He was so shocked that he made no effort to escape. They roped and added him to the collection.

'You'll all hang for helpin' kidnap Van Avery and Mrs. Steele,' Hashknife told him.

The guard's expression was comically blank.

'Somebody is shore crazy,' he said.

'If they ain't, they will be.' Hashknife chuckled as he and Sleepy went out and back to their horses.

For several minutes the prisoners tried to loosen their bonds, but uselessly.

Ortelle lay back, panting weakly.

'That was Hartley,' he told them. 'He was thrown into that old Kelley tunnel, and they blew down the hill on him. I tell you, I saw it and—and a gopher couldn't have dug out. He can't be out. There ain't no way for him to *ever* get out.'

'You damn little fool!' roared one of the men. 'Do you think a ghost could tie knots like these?'

'I—I can't help it. I've seen that cave-in, and I know. I wish I had my glasses.'

'To hell with your glasses! Where they'll put you, you won't need glasses. What about that kidnapin', eh?'

'I don't know,' wailed Ortelle. 'They can't charge us with that.'

'No? Hartley couldn't git out—but he is out.'

'He couldn't,' wailed Ortelle. 'I can take you out there and show you why he couldn't.'

'All right, I'll go with you. I'd give every hunk of gold I ever higraded, and every other cent I ever had, jist to be that far away from this damn place right now.'

'Well, you ain't goin',' said the guard. 'Take your medicine. Unless I'm damn badly mistaken, there's goin' to be plenty company.'

'We ain't done nothin' but higrade,' said another. 'That is, all except Ortelle. He's been sort of a active member, you might say.'

But Ortelle had nothing to say. He stared at the pile of gold ore on the tarpaulin and wondered how a man could be sealed up in a mine and still be outside and able to tie knots.

The Yucca Saloon was crowded that evening. Silver Steele and Rick Nelson had decided to hold a mass meeting to see what could be done about the way things were going in the county; and they had decided to hold it in the Yucca. Ken Steele was there, his head swathed in bandages.

There had been much drinking that day, and the meeting was noisy.

'I don't see how you can accomplish much,' said the sheriff. 'It's been talked over all day, and there ain't been a damn one offered a suggestion.'

'And another thing,' added Handsome, 'you don't know how many right in here belong to the bad bunch. I tell you, I suspect everybody—even Banty.'

Steele was also dubious of any good resulting from a mass meeting.

'But we've got to do somethin',' he said. 'A poor start is better than no start at all. What's your idea, Rick?'

Nelson thought it over grimly.

'As you say, we've got to make some kind of a start. Ault thought it might be a good idea for everybody to keep watch real close; and if they got anything to work on, let the committee know it. He thought a committee of five ought to be plenty. Say, Ault, Steele, and myself, for three, and let the crowd pick the other two. Might include the sheriff, as far as that goes.'

'Why report to any damn committee?' asked Handsome. 'Believe me, if I got any kind of a line on them killers, Saint Peter would have to appoint a committee to ask 'em questions. The thing to do is to shoot first and ask questions afterward. Mebbe we'd start another Boot Hill, but we'd soon clean 'em up.'

Silver Steele managed to call the meeting to order. He recited the things that had happened, beginning with the ore-stealing at the Comanche Chief and the murder of Payzant, and making a brief summary of it all down to the kidnaping of Gladys Steele and Van Avery. Steele was a good talker, and the crowd listened to him. They laughed at the efforts of the bad bunch to kill off Van Avery, thinking he was a detective. By the time Steele finished talking, they were ready to do anything to stop the murder and robbery in Painted Wells.

McCord shifted nervously. He wondered why Ike Berry didn't come back. There had been plenty of time for Ike to make that round trip to Porcupine. McCord wasn't worried about that stolen horse. And another thing bothered McCord—the box stolen from the freight wagon.

His eyes often shifted to Rick Nelson and Ed Ault.

Rick Nelson's speech was but a repetition of Steele's talk. Steele had told it all, and Nelson was only able to drive a few points home. He dilated on the murder of Dave Bush. Dave had been with him for a long time, and he hungered for a chance to put a rope around the necks of the men who murdered him.

There was no speakers' platform. The men lounged against the bar, sat on the tables and chairs—even on the bar rail. Ed Ault stepped out from the bar, taking Rick Nelson's place, as Nelson finished. And almost at the same moment Sleepy Stevens sauntered through the front door and came in at the rear of the crowd.

Some of the men moved aside to give Sleepy room, but he stopped at the end of the bar near the door, looking lazily around. He caught Handsome's eye, and the deputy edged back to him. Sleepy's lips barely moved, but Handsome caught the words, 'Look out.'

Casually his hands hitched his belt around a little. Banty Brayton was watching them. His eyes flashed around the room, and he dropped one hand to his side. The crowd seemed tense as Ault began speaking. His voice was a little husky.

'Men, we've got to clean up this country,' he said. 'You've heard Steele and Nelson. I can't add much to their talks. In fact, I can't add anythin'. I'd be—'

'Oh, yes, you could, Ault.'

The voice was knife-edged, pitched in a conversational key; but it fairly crackled in that smoke-filled room.

Then came a sibilant hiss of indrawn breath, a choking curse.

Standing between them and the open rear door, like a gray ghost in the smoke, his long, lean face barely distinguishable beneath the low brim of his sombrero, stood Hashknife Hartley.

His head did not move as his keen eyes flashed from man to man.

'Lord!' choked a voice. It was Steve McCord.

Ault's jaw was sagging; he swayed weakly. The dead had come back.

A man, panting heavily, shoved in at the front door, stopping within a pace of Sleepy. It was Ike Berry.

'Hello, Fillmore,' said Hashknife.

Berry jerked up his head, his face blanching.

'Steve, look out!' he screamed. 'They got Brad!'

His right hand reached for his gun, but Sleepy's gun had swung up, flashed down, and Ike Berry fell in a huddle on the floor.

But many of the men did not see Berry; they were watching Hashknife.

'Ault! Nelson! McCord!' Hashknife snapped their names. 'Thatcher is dead. Ortelle is all tied up for shipment. The game is over.'

McCord came out of his trance like a trapped wolf. Ghost or no ghost, he knew too much.

Men dodged back. But McCord's gun-hand had lost its cunning. He shot once, his bullet striking a rack of pool balls three feet wide of Hashknife. Then McCord doubled up and went down. The ghost rarely missed.

Nelson was not game in a pinch. He sprang back, intending to reach the rear door; but he crashed into Silver Steele, who tripped him, and they went down with a tremendous crash.

Ault didn't move as Hashknife came in close and shoved the muzzle of his gun against the gambler's ribs. He seemed hypnotized, unable to move. Other men helped Silver Steele hold the struggling Nelson, who was mouthing curses and denials as fast as he could talk.

Handsome put handcuffs on Ike Berry; but Ike didn't mind because he was still asleep from the blow Sleepy had given him with his gun.

'Talk fast, Ault,' gritted Hashknife. 'Where are they—down in Nelson's basement?'

Ault's frightened eyes shifted to the amazed crowd. He seemed unable to speak.

'Go ahead and talk,' repeated Hashknife.

Ault drew a deep breath.

'Yes,' he whispered, and grabbed at his throat as if unable to get his breath.

Hashknife did not turn his head as he said—

'Mrs. Ken Steele and Van Avery are in the basement under Nelson's assay office.'

Ken Steele and his father were the first ones out of the place. Nelson was slumped down in a chair, quivering from fright and rage; but he was through making denials. The sheriff, his hands shaking, was putting handcuffs on Ed Ault. The reaction was almost too much for the sheriff of Painted Wells. It was difficult for him to believe that Hashknife was anything but a ghost.

They let Ault sit down in a chair. He had a gun in his coat-pocket, but had made no move to draw it.

'Feel like talkin'?' asked Hashknife.

Ault licked his lips and shook his head.

238

'Where in Heaven's name did you come from, Hashknife?' asked the sheriff.

'Oh, I've been around some. A number of these pleasant gentlemen knocked me out, put me in an old tunnel up there beyond the Comanche Chief, and then dynamited the old timbers. Buried me alive. And that was their mistake; they should have buried me dead.'

A cheer sounded across the street, and Hashknife guessed that Gladys and Blondy had been found. Ault slumped lower in his chair, his eyes staring at Steve McCord, who had not moved.

Some of the crowd was coming back into the Yucca, and with them was Van Avery, hardly able to walk, his lips stiff from the tight gag he had been wearing. His eyes laughed, but the lower part of his face was a frozen mask. Silver Steele was with them.

'They're all right!' he yelled. 'We found 'em both down there in the dark, tied up tight and gagged.'

Steele strode in close and looked down at Ault, who refused to look up.

'Damn you, Ault,' said Steele bitterly, 'you pulled that job! Gladys tore your mask off at the ranch, and you had to take her along. That alone would hang you.'

But Ault made no comment. Steele turned to Hashknife.

'How did you do it, Hartley?' he asked huskily.

'Think of it! Ault, Nelson, and McCord! Why, they were goin' to head our vigilante gang. No wonder they froze at the sight of you. I thought you was a ghost; and I can imagine what they thought.'

'I reckon I did give 'em a little shock,' Hashknife smiled. 'But they had a shock comin'. You've got to give a lot of credit to Sleepy and Van Avery. When you're playin' ghost, you've got to have a lot of mediums workin' for you.'

But the crowd was impatient. They wanted to know things. Here was Steve McCord, pumped full of lead; Ike Berry, unconscious and handcuffed; Nelson, cursing everybody and everything, and Ault, as collapsed as a pin-pricked toy balloon.

They understood that Ken Steele's wife had torn the mask off Ault's face, and that Ault was implicated in the kidnaping; but they wanted to know why these things had been done. The prosecuting attorney, red-faced and puffing, shoved his way in. He had gathered scattered bits of what had happened.

Hashknife touched Ed Ault on the shoulder, but the gambler did not look up.

'A little talk can't hurt you, Ault,' said Hashknife. 'I've got the whole story, anyway. Thatcher killed Milt Corey, didn't he?'

Ault nodded.

'Ike Berry's right name is Fillmore, and he was

the man who done all the safe-crackin' for you.'

'Well?' choked Ault. 'You seem to know it all.'

'Who killed Payzant?'

'Rick Nelson.'

'You damn dirty liar!' screamed Nelson. 'You was as much in that as I was. And I never killed him. Dave Bush hit him first, and all I done was—What do you want to tell so much for? Let 'em try to prove it.'

The prosecuting attorney laughed cacklingly, and Nelson swore at him.

'You never went to Phoenix, Ault,' said Hashknife. 'You bought a ticket for Phoenix, but you got off at Porcupine. Then you helped the boys smash that safe at the Comanche Chief mine. I've got Ortelle and three other men all tied up at the mine. Ortelle loaded that gun for Ryan, didn't he?'

'Yes, I told the fool to get rid of that gun.'

'And Ike Berry tried to kill Judge Frazer because he knew the old lawyer recognized him, eh?'

Ault nodded, his eyes on the floor. The crowd had massed around them, gasping at Hashknife's uncanny knowledge of what had been done.

'You had quite an organization, Ault. You made a lot of money. Higradin' the Comanche Chief wasn't enough for you, though. Do you know you made an awful mistake in killin' Dave Bush. You thought he double-crossed you on that bank robbery money; so you shot him down for it. Pretty slick. You sent a swamper over to Nelson's store to buy kerosene after dark; and you had gunmen planted to git him when he went out to the storage shed.'

Ault looked up at Hashknife, his face ashen.

'For God's sake, do you know everything?' he asked huskily.

'I know plenty. I know where that money is, and the bank will get it all back. I wonder if you know where you made your biggest mistake? Well, one was when you gave me a chance to git out of that tunnel; but your really big one was when you gave Doc Smedley a chance to take that bullet out of Bill Neer's dead body.

'It was solid gold, Ault; a solid gold .45-70 bullet. Dipped 'em in quicksilver to make 'em look like lead, didn't you? I wondered why Neer would be unloadin' a rifle cartridge. Gold bullets are rare things, Ault.

'By the way, what was the idea of leavin' powder in them cartridges when you reloaded 'em with gold bullets?'

'That was Bush's fool idea,' said Ault. 'He wanted 'em real, and he loaded a lot of 'em that way, before Nelson made him leave the powder out. Bush was afraid somebody might get one by mistake and try to shoot it.'

'I never did see a gold bullet,' said Silver Steele.

'Well, I've got a whole case of 'em hidden down in the brush along the road,' said Hashknife. 'I stole 'em off Steve McCord's wagon.

He was takin' 'em to Porcupine, where he'd cook 'em down in his own molds and send 'em to the mint from the Hellbender mine.

'Our fussy friend, Mr. Nelson over there, ran the gold into bullets in his basement, and handed 'em over the counter to the X8X cow outfit. If anybody got suspicious and examined their load, all they'd find would be innocent-lookin' cartridges.'

Silver Steele snorted out loud. It was clear enough to him now.

'I reckon Steve McCord wasn't so awful worried about them shells, 'cause he thought mebbe Brad Thatcher had stolen 'em. Well, I don't mind tellin' you that Brad Thatcher ain't goin' to steal no more. And here's somethin' for Mr. Rick Nelson to chew on. It'll interest Mr. Ault, too. Mr. Nelson struck some mighty rich ore on that prospect where Payzant was killed. The vein dipped in under Corey's property; so Mr. Nelson schemed to get that property. As long as Milt Corey was alive, he'd block Mr. Nelson; so they killed Mr. Corey, stole back the ten thousand dollars, breaking the Diamond C; and they intended buyin' the place from the bank. If that vein holds good, I don't reckon the Corey family will be broke long. I guess Payzant found out what I did, and they killed him. They tried to kill me, but it didn't take.'

The crowd parted to let in the Corey family. Ma

Corey was in the lead, and she came straight to Hashknife. For several moments she held both his hands, and then reached up and kissed him. She turned to the crowd, her eyes full of tears.

'I've never been in a saloon before,' she sobbed. 'I never kissed any man, except my husband and my son-in-law. But right now I could kiss all of you.'

Hashknife laughed and put his arm around her.

'That's all right,' he said. 'I shore appreciate that kiss.'

'And Ken has been cleared?' asked Elene. 'Somebody said—'

'You betcha!' exclaimed Handsome. 'Clean as a dollar.'

Elene turned to Hashknife, her eyes shining.

'You've been wonderful,' she said softly. 'Just wonderful.'

'Aw, shucks, I never done anythin', Elene.'

'Do I have to climb up on something to kiss you?'

'Bend over, cowboy,' gurgled Van Avery. 'That's the stuff!'

Hashknife's leathery face was as red as a beet, but he gave Elene a hug and whispered in her ear—

'Don't forget that Blondy was my big helper.'

'I won't,' she whispered.

Hashknife turned to the sheriff:

'Banty, if you'll look in the brush jist off to the

right of where I turned that freight wagon around down there, you'll find a case of rifle cartridges with gold bullets. And down in the cellar of the Corey house, under the cot, you'll find that sack of money which belongs to the bank.'

Hashknife looked old and weary as he walked to the doorway. Silver Steele gripped his hand, but did not say anything. Blondy Van Avery was speaking, and Hashknife stopped to listen.

'Everybody around here thought I was a detective,' he said. 'I suppose some of you thought I acted a fool to disguise myself. But I didn't; I merely acted natural. My name is really Van Avery.

'You see, Jim Payzant was my uncle, and I thought a lot of him. He was sort of an ideal to me, because I've always wanted to be a detective. I was in San Francisco when I heard of his death; so I came out here to see if I couldn't find out who killed him.

'But I don't want to be a detective now. I just want to stay here. I've got some great ideas. In fact, I've had a great idea ever since I got on that train at Porcupine, with some of Steve McCord's gang shooting at me through the window. My idea was right there on that train, and'—Van Avery grinned foolishly—'I've been working with that idea in mind ever since. As Sleepy Stevens would say "I'm scared to death that everythin' is goin' to be all right."'

Elene's face was red now, but she smiled at Van Avery, as he put his arm around Mrs. Corey's shoulder.

Hashknife stepped outside. Sleepy met him, and without a word they went out to their horses. Mounting quickly, they circled away from the main street and headed south. Their job was over and they were going away.

'We'll pick up our warbags at the ranch,' said Hashknife, as they struck the road below town.

'Shore,' agreed Sleepy.

They rode along silently for a mile.

'Got a match?' asked Sleepy.

He scratched the match on the leg of his chaps and looked at a slip of yellow paper. Just a glance and he flipped the match away.

'It's made out to you, pardner,' he said.

'What's made out to me?' asked Hashknife.

'Silver Steele's check for ten thousand dollars.'

'I wish he hadn't done that,' said Hashknife slowly. 'Ten thousand! More money than we ever expected to own in the world. Still, I wish he hadn't done that.'

'So do I,' said Sleepy. 'I shore wish he hadn't done that.'

Hashknife chuckled softly.

'You liar.'

'I'm not—honest. I wish he hadn't.'

'Hadn't what, Sleepy?'

'Why, made it out to you, of course.'

And they rode knee to knee down the dusty highway, free to do as they pleased. The tall hills were calling again.

Center Point Large Print
600 Brooks Road / PO Box 1
Thorndike, ME 04986-0001 USA

(207) 568-3717

US & Canada:
1 800 929-9108
www.centerpointlargeprint.com